Zoe popped the stud on her hot pants

The small sound brought Liam's gaze to her waist. She had a sudden flash of how it had been all those years ago, the way he'd slid his hand under the waistband of her jeans at first rather than undo her fly, how she'd had to beg him to touch her properly.

The memory urged her on as she slid her zipper down.

"Don't." His voice sounded too loud in the small space. A muscle jumped in his jaw.

Good. She wanted him to sweat. Once, she'd begged him to love her and he'd pushed her out the door then abandoned her without a word. Tonight she was the one in charge.

She pushed the hot pants down her legs and stepped out of them, standing in front of him in nothing but her black lace thong and bra and her red garters and stockings.

"So what's it going to be, Liam? Are you going to give me what I need?"

She'd always imagined what it would be like to be with him. She'd been so desperate for him years ago that she'd begged him to take her virginity. But he'd pushed her away and left her wanting.

Not this time. Not if she had any say in the matter...

Blaze™

Dear Reader,

I had the beginning for this story years ago, and it
has been percolating away in my subconscious ever
since: a man walks into an art gallery and sees a
portrait of a beautiful, naked woman and recognizes
her as the great lost love of his life. I could almost see
this moment in my mind like a scene from a movie.
But for many years I had no idea what came after
that moment, what kind of man he was, and what
kind of woman she was.

Well, now I know. Liam is a bad boy, and Zoe is
the perfect bad girl to help heal his wounded heart.
Because they're both so stubborn, their journey to
love is a fiery and passionate one. I hope you enjoy
reading it and watching them learn to trust again.

I love hearing from readers, so if you'd like to drop
me a line or find out more about me and my books,
please visit my Web site at www.sarahmayberry.com.

Happy reading!

Sarah Mayberry

She's Got It Bad

SARAH MAYBERRY

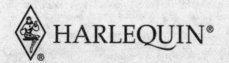

HARLEQUIN®

TORONTO • NEW YORK • LONDON
AMSTERDAM • PARIS • SYDNEY • HAMBURG
STOCKHOLM • ATHENS • TOKYO • MILAN • MADRID
PRAGUE • WARSAW • BUDAPEST • AUCKLAND

Recycling programs
for this product may
not exist in your area.

ISBN-13: 978-0-373-79468-3
ISBN-10:   0-373-79468-1

SHE'S GOT IT BAD

www.eHarlequin.com

Printed in U.S.A.

ABOUT THE AUTHOR

Sarah Mayberry has recently decided to list her profession as Gypsy/writer, since she's moved eight times in the past five years. Currently she's based in Auckland, New Zealand, but she still calls Melbourne, Australia, home and hopes to have a latte on Brunswick Street sometime soon. When she's not writing books, she also writes for TV, reads, cooks, shops for shoes and tries to get her derriere to the gym occasionally.

Books by Sarah Mayberry

HARLEQUIN BLAZE
211—CAN'T GET ENOUGH
251—CRUISE CONTROL*
278—ANYTHING FOR YOU*
314—TAKE ON ME**
320—ALL OVER YOU**
326—HOT FOR HIM**
380—BURNING UP
404—BELOW THE BELT
425—AMOROUS LIAISONS

HARLEQUIN
SUPERROMANCE
1551—A NATURAL FATHER

*It's All About Attitude
**Secret Lives of Daytime Divas

Every book is a journey, and I wouldn't have been able to take this one without Chris holding my hand, as always. I love you.

Then there is my editor, the amazing and talented Wanda, who always steers me right—thank you for listening to me ramble and curse and always, somehow, managing to sound interested no matter how long it goes on.

And lastly, thanks to Mihiteria, for helping me keep writing and laughing even when sometimes it felt like an uphill battle.

Prologue

Melbourne, Australia
October 1997

IT WAS SO DARK that Liam Masters could barely see his hand in front of his face. His boots scuffed against an uneven stretch of concrete as he turned from the Fords' driveway onto the paved path that led through their backyard. He could just make out the paleness of the studio ahead, a less-dark shape in all the blackness.

If he'd stayed at the party, he'd probably be peeling off Sally Kendrick's underwear by now. At seventeen, he had more than enough experience to know when he was going to get lucky.

He had no idea why he'd decided to come home instead.

Stupid, that's what he was.

A shadow moved against the side of the studio as he reached into his pocket for his keys. He froze, muscles tensing. Then he heard someone take a deep, shaky breath and the smell of honeysuckle reached him on the warm night air.

Zoe.

He pushed his hands into his back pockets. The safest place for them when Zoe Ford was around.

"You're home early," she said.

"What are you doing out here?" His voice came out sharper, harder than he'd intended.

"Waiting for you."

He didn't know what to do with her straight-up answer.

"You shouldn't be out here," he said. "What if Tom comes home?"

Her brother was wildly protective of her. Liam didn't need to see her face to know that she was frowning. Could picture her dark eyebrows knitting together, the stubbornness in her green eyes.

"I'm sick of waiting," she said.

Shit.

He wished he hadn't downed those three beers at the party. His brain was fuzzy, not as crisp as he needed it to be when he was within touching distance of his best friend's little sister.

"No one asked you to wait," he said.

They weren't talking about him coming home from the party to find her on the front step of his temporary home. They both knew that.

"Is it true?" she asked.

"What?"

"What Tom told me. Is it true you're going out with Sally Kendrick?"

"You need to go inside before your parents hear us," he said.

"Are you going out with her or not?" Zoe's voice was shaking.

"No."

He should have lied. Told her he and Sally were nuts about each other, that he'd just rolled out of her bed.

"Is that why you're home early? Because things didn't work out with Sally?"

She'd moved closer, within reach. He could see the pale oval of her face, smell the sweet honeysuckle smell of her favorite body lotion.

She's fifteen, man. Fifteen, and the daughter of the people who took you in when no one else wanted you.

He needed to make her go inside, back to her own bedroom, back to her single bed and her walls covered with posters of heavy-metal bands and football teams.

"I don't know why I came home," he said.

She took another step closer. What little light there was glinted off her eyes.

"Kiss me," she said. "Please."

He clenched his hands into the denim of his jeans.

"You have to go inside." His voice sounded low and too quiet. Unconvincing. Desperate.

She must have thought so, too, because she took a last step and closed the distance between them. He could feel the warmth of her body, the brush of her small, firm breasts against his chest, the whisper of her breath on his neck.

"I can't stand it anymore, Liam. Sitting opposite you at breakfast and dinner, seeing you at school, at home. I can't stop thinking about you. Please kiss me."

Every muscle in his body tensed as she slid her arms around his waist. She pressed her body against his, her hands clutching at his back. She lifted her head, and her hair skimmed his chin as she pressed tentative kisses onto his collarbone and neck. One, two, three, her mouth soft and moist.

He was already hard. Had been since the moment he caught the scent of honeysuckle. She pressed her hips against his and the pressure made him groan.

"No," he said, reaching for her shoulders to push her away.

But somehow he was sliding his hands into her hair instead, holding her head and tilting her face toward him. Then he was kissing her, his tongue in her mouth, her taste surrounding him.

She'd never been kissed before. He knew because she'd told

him two months ago. He'd been thinking about being her first ever since. He wanted to make his mark on her, make it perfect.

He stroked her tongue with his and traced her lower lip before sucking it into his mouth. She made a small sobbing sound and angled her head to give him more access. She tasted so sweet, so clean and sweet.

He slid a hand down her back to cup her backside, holding her against himself as he flexed his hips forward, feeling her mound against his erection.

He was so hard. Man, he wanted… He wanted so much he was afraid he was about to lose it.

Her hands were tugging at the bottom of his T-shirt.

"Take this off. I want to touch you," she said.

She yanked the T-shirt up and he released his grip on her long enough for her to pull it over his head. Then her hands were on him, touching, smoothing, teasing, discovering.

He couldn't think. Didn't want to. As her fingers found his nipples, he broke their kiss long enough to pull his keys from his pocket. His hand was shaking so much it was a miracle he got the key in the lock. Then he was kissing her again and backing her up the few stairs and inside the studio toward his bed.

She stopped when the backs of her knees hit the mattress.

"Wait," she said, and he heard the rustle of clothing and knew she'd tugged off her own T-shirt.

He swore under his breath. She never wore a bra, even though her mom hassled her about it. He'd wanted to touch her, hold her for so long now. Wanted to know what color her nipples were, if they were as sweet and plump as they looked through the fabric of her T-shirts.

"Zoe, I have to see you."

He flicked the bedside lamp on and she blinked in the sudden light. Her hands came up to cover herself. He reached for them and slowly tugged them away, holding her arms out from her sides.

He sucked in a breath when he saw her, so pink and firm. Her nipples were like little berries, hard already even though he hadn't touched them yet.

"Zoe," he said, reaching for her.

She shuddered as he slid his hands up her torso. She felt like warm silk, so smooth and perfect. His palms covered her breasts, his thumbs finding her nipples. She bit her lip as he teased them.

"That feels so good," she whispered, her eyes half-closed.

She looked beautiful standing there in nothing but her jeans and bare feet, her long dark hair spilling down her back, her cheeks and chest flushed. He ducked his head and kissed her again, his hands teasing all the while. She started to press her pelvis forward and he could feel her heart pounding. He ducked his head and kissed his way down her neck to her chest until he was pulling one hard little nipple into his mouth.

"Oh," she said. Her body jerked in his arms. Her hands found his head, her fingers burrowing into his hair as she held him at her breast, her breath coming in sharp pants. "So good, Liam, so good," she whispered over and over.

He pushed her back onto the bed and they fell together. He relished the feel of her beneath him, loving the way she instinctively opened her thighs so that he could press his hardness against the hot heart of her.

They kissed and grabbed at each other for long minutes, hips grinding together through two layers of denim, the friction exquisite but not nearly enough.

He slid a hand over her mound and found the thick seam where her jeans joined at the crotch. He pressed firmly, feeling how hot and steamy she was. Her hands grabbed at his shoulders and her hips lifted.

"Liam," she said. "Yes."

He rubbed her some more, and she circled her hips, her eyes closed as she gave herself over to the moment.

He wanted inside her so bad. He slid a hand to the waistband of her jeans, slipped his fingers beneath the fabric. She caught her breath and he felt her belly tense beneath his hand. Then she was widening her legs, encouraging him to keep going. He slid his hand farther, into her soft curls. She stilled as he sent a single finger probing lower.

Man, she was so wet. Hot and slippery and wet. He pressed his hard-on against her thigh as his finger slid between her folds.

"Liam!" she said. "That is… That is unbelievable!"

He grinned at the shocked expression on her face then watched her closely as he slicked a finger over the hard little button hidden between her folds. She shuddered, her breasts rising dramatically as she pulled in a lungful of air.

"Don't stop," she begged. "Whatever you're doing, don't stop."

He lowered his head and took a nipple into his mouth, his finger sliding over and over her, delving deeper, lower with each rotation until, finally, he was at her hot entrance and she was tilting her hips in wordless invitation.

He sucked hard on her nipple as he slid his finger inside her. Slick, hot muscle closed around him, so tight and wet he groaned.

"Take your jeans off. I want to see you. I want to touch you," Zoe panted.

She drove her fingers into his hair and dragged his head up from her breasts so he was forced to look her in the eye.

"I want you to be my first, Liam. I want to sleep with you," she said.

His hard-on throbbed at the thought of being inside her,

taking what she was so generously, passionately, warmly offering.

He loved her. She was so beautiful. Never more so than right at this moment, with her eyes clouded with desire and her face flushed.

"I want to touch you," she said again. His hand stilled between her legs as she slid her own hand down his body to where his cock was pressed against her thigh. He closed his eyes as she smoothed her hand along his length, her caress firm through his jeans.

"I don't care about anything else. I just want you. I've always wanted you," she said.

"I've always wanted you," he said as her fingers found the stud on his jeans. She popped it free and pulled his zipper down. He held his breath as her hand worked its way inside his jeans.

She found him, her fingers encircling him, tentative at first but with more confidence as she felt how hard he was, how much he wanted her.

"How can it be so soft and so hard at the same time?" she asked.

"How can you be so hot and so wet?"

She laughed and smoothed her hand up and down his shaft. He began to move his finger again, slicking over and over her. She dropped her head back and lifted her hips.

"Please, Liam. Please," she begged.

He didn't know why he wasn't tearing her jeans off, why he wasn't inside her already. This was his every fantasy come true—beautiful, sleek, sweet Zoe in his bed, panting for him, her hands on him, pleading with him to take her. How many times had he lain here in the dark of night, his hand wrapped around his own hardness as he imagined her begging like this, imagined the taste of her, the feel of her?

Too many. Almost every night since he'd moved in with the Fords after his mom died. A whole year.

She made a disgruntled noise when he pulled his hand free from her jeans but she smiled when he popped her jeans open and his fingers found the tab on her zipper.

"Yes. Finally!" she said as he tugged it down.

She was wearing plain white panties with some kind of writing on them. It wasn't until she was lifting her hips to help him slide them off that he realized what they said.

Friday's Child Is Loving and Giving.

He stilled, the only sound his harsh breathing as he stared at the words, emblazoned across the plumpness of her mons, the darkness of her pubic hair showing faintly through the thin white cotton.

Loving and giving. That was exactly what Zoe was. She was also smart, brave, stubborn. She could sketch and draw like no one he'd ever known, and she never backed off from a challenge. Never wore skirts, either, or makeup. Knew how to change the starter motor in her father's old Mini. How to throw a cricket ball and kick a football.

She had no idea how gorgeous she was. How many of the guys at school watched her when she walked past in her jeans and T-shirts with no bra. Her green eyes, the perfect oval of her face, the dimple in her chin. In a few years' time, she was going to understand how much she was worth, how precious she was.

"Liam," she said, wiggling her hips impatiently. "Hurry up!"

She was going to regret this moment. After all, who was he? Liam Masters, thick as two planks if his teachers were to be believed. Homeless, parentless. Alone, destined for nothing. Staying here with the Fords was the first lucky break he'd had in his life. He didn't expect it to last, or to change anything, despite how hard Mrs. Ford was campaigning for him to repeat a year so he could get better marks and apply to university.

He knew who he was, what he was. He'd learned it young, at his father's knee.

There was no way he was good enough for Zoe Ford. Certainly not good enough to be her first.

"What? What's wrong?" Zoe propped herself up on both elbows to stare at him.

"I can't do this."

He grabbed the waistband of her jeans and pulled them up. She resisted, a frown on her face.

"What? What do you mean? I don't understand."

"We're not going to do this, Zoe. You need to get dressed and go back to the house."

She stared at him, her mouth open. He could see the hurt in her eyes as desire was replaced by confusion.

"Did I— Did I do something wrong?" she asked. "Tell me what to do, what to say, and I'll do it, Liam."

"You need to get dressed," he said again.

He tugged the two sides of her jeans together and pulled up the zipper. She pushed his hands away from the stud when he went to close it.

"I don't understand what's happening," she said.

There were tears in her eyes. She pushed herself backward on the bed and pulled her knees up to her chest. "Liam, please. Don't do this."

"This is a big mistake. I'm doing you a favor," he said.

He tucked himself back into his jeans and zipped himself up. Then he stood at the end of the bed, looking down at her.

"You need to go before someone catches you in here," he said.

She blinked away tears. "Is that what you're worried about? Someone finding us? Because I would never tell, Liam. I love you. You know that. I'd never get you in trouble."

"You're fifteen, Zoe. Tom trusts me, your parents trust me. They took me in."

She shook her head. "Bull. This isn't about my parents or my brother. Tell me what's really wrong. Is it because I'm a virgin? Or is it my boobs? I know they're small but I didn't think you'd mind. Mom said they'll get bigger as I get older…"

Liam swore under his breath and raked a hand through his hair.

"It's nothing to do with you, Zoe. It's me, okay? You don't want me to be your first."

"I do. More than anything."

She stared at him with her big trusting eyes, so earnest and open and honest.

"You have no idea who I really am." He thought of the girls he'd slept with, the fights he'd had, the things he'd stolen, the lies he'd told. He thought of him and his mom escaping into the night with their lives crammed into a single black garbage bag thanks to his old man. "You don't want me."

Zoe shook her head. "I do. You're the only one I want."

She swung her legs over the edge of the bed and stood. Her arms were crossed over her chest as she moved to stand in front of him. She bared herself so that she could reach for his hands, pulling them toward her.

"I want you. See?" she said, pressing his hands against her breasts.

Her eyes, her face pleaded with him. He felt the warm softness of her beneath his hands. Wanted so much to haul her to him and take what she was offering.

He forced himself to keep his hands unresponsive, to push her away instead of drawing her closer. She gasped.

He stooped to grab her T-shirt.

"Get dressed," he said.

She just stared at him, her arms once more crossed protectively.

"I love you, Liam," she said. "Please don't do this."

"You'll thank me one day," he said.

He dropped the T-shirt onto the end of the bed and turned his back on her, walking to the window so he wouldn't have to look at her a second longer. He would never forget how she looked, standing there with her eyes so full of pain and confusion.

The rush of movement and the sound of the door slamming signaled her exit. He closed his eyes.

So close. He'd come so close to taking something that wasn't his. Something perfect.

He crossed to the bed and sat on the edge, his head in his hands. Images from the past few minutes flashed across his mind. Zoe's breasts, damp from where he'd kissed her. Her eyes, heavy with need. The hitch in her breathing when he'd slid his hand between her legs.

He knew what he had to do. He pulled out the duffel bag from beneath his bed. It didn't take him long to pack. Life had taught him to travel light. He hesitated a moment before grabbing the photograph he kept hidden in the biker magazines beside his bed. Tom and him and Zoe, laughing last summer as they attacked each other with water pistols. He slid it into his back pocket then headed for the door.

His motorbike was in the garage and he wheeled it carefully past Mr. Ford's Mini and Mrs. Ford's sensible Volvo wagon. He propped it on its stand at the end of the driveway in the circle of light from a streetlamp and settled in to wait for Tom to come home.

Liam was stiff and his ass was numb from sitting on the cold concrete curb before Tom turned the corner at two in the morning. Liam stood as his friend stopped in front of him, a smile on his face.

"Mate. What are you doing out here?" Tom was hazy-eyed, a bit drunk. "Why'd you leave so early, you bastard?

Party was just getting started. Sally was mighty pissed with you, let me tell you."

Then he registered Liam's bike, the duffel bag strapped on the back. His smile faded.

"What's going on?"

"I'm heading off. Time to move on," Liam said.

Tom frowned. "What? What do you mean?"

"Don't want to overstay my welcome," Liam said with a shrug.

"No way. You can't go like this. Mom'll freak out. Dad'll have a cow. God knows what Zoe will do. You know she worships the ground you freakin' walk on."

Liam pulled the letter he'd written from his back pocket. It wasn't much—a bare thanks, a thin explanation, plus all the cash he had on him to pay for his bills to date. It would have to do.

Tom stared at the envelope, refusing to take it.

"I can't believe you're serious. What happened? Have you heard from your dad? If he's hassling you, we can go to the cops," Tom said.

"I just have to go."

Tom stared at him, his green eyes, so like Zoe's, searching Liam's face. Then he crossed to the bike and tugged the keys from the ignition, sliding them into his pocket.

"Hey!"

"Tell me what happened and I'll give them back," Tom said.

"Nothing happened."

"Bull."

"Give me the keys, Tom. All you need to know is that I'm doing the right thing."

"Sneaking off in the middle of the night? Yeah, really noble."

"Give me the keys." Liam moved forward, but Tom backed away.

"Tell me what's going on."

Liam swore and lunged at his friend. Tom dodged to the side.

"Tom…" Liam warned.

He lunged again, and again Tom slipped away.

"Tell me."

"No."

"Tell me."

Liam feinted to the left then grabbed a handful of Tom's shirt when he tried to veer right. They wrestled in silence, grabbing fistfuls of each other's clothing, not wanting to hurt each other. After a few minutes they broke apart. They eyed each other, fighting for breath. The words were in Liam's throat and out his mouth before he could think twice.

"It's Zoe," he said. "I can't stay because of Zoe."

Tom frowned. "Because she's got a crush on you? I know she can be a pain, but it's not that bad…"

Liam stared at him, letting the silence grow. Tom jerked his head in sudden realization.

"No way," he said, shaking his head.

"Nothing happened."

Tom took a step away, then stepped forward again, still shaking his head.

"You and my sister? Tell me this is a joke."

Liam knew what Tom was thinking. He'd heard Liam talk about girls, knew he'd had more than his fair share over the past few years. Knew Liam never stayed long after he got what he wanted.

"Nothing happened. I sent her back to the house before things got out of hand."

"Jesus! What the hell was she doing alone with you anyway? How long has this been going on for?"

Liam shook his head. "It hasn't. I mean, I've always liked her. But I've never touched her before."

Tom swore and threw his hands in the air. "You touched my sister?"

"I didn't screw her, if that's what you're thinking," Liam said.

Tom's fist came out of nowhere, connecting with Liam's jaw and sending a flash of white pain up the side of his face. He staggered, then shook his head to clear the ringing in his ears.

"You asshole. Dammit, you asshole," Tom said. "She's fifteen. Fifteen!"

Liam held his ground. "That's why I'm going."

Tom dug his hand into his pocket. Liam caught a flash of silver as his motorbike keys flew toward his head. He was too slow to react and they grazed his cheekbone before hitting the ground. He felt a trickle of warmth on his face as he bent to retrieve them.

He offered Tom the letter again, but his friend eyed him coldly. Liam crossed to the mailbox and slid the envelope inside. It would have to do.

"For what it's worth, I love her," he said as he reached for his helmet.

Tom turned his back and walked up the driveway. Liam watched until he disappeared from sight, then rocked his bike off its stand and wheeled it to the end of the street.

The bike roared to life, the motor throbbing between his thighs. He didn't look back as he twisted the throttle and sped down the street.

He'd made the right decision. He knew he had.

1

Twelve Years Later

LIAM FINGERED the single button on his jacket as he approached the well-lit entrance of Hartman's Art Gallery. A woman in her thirties waited in the foyer, tall and elegant. Her platinum-blond bob swung around her jaw as she turned to face him, a welcoming smile on her face.

"Liam. You came," Jacinta Hartman said.

"Of course."

Her smile faded as she registered his clothes.

"You're not wearing the tie I bought you."

"Nope."

"Liam…"

He held out his arms to draw attention to the well-cut wool trousers, jacket and crisply tailored shirt he was wearing.

"Come on, cut me some slack here. Not an inch of denim or leather in sight," he said.

"And you're not wearing your beautiful new shoes, either," she said, eyeing his favorite boots unhappily.

He slid an arm around her slim waist and pulled her close.

"I said you could try to civilize me. I didn't say it would work," he reminded her. He kissed her and she pulled back before he could smear her lipstick.

"Liam, people can see us," she said.

Which made him laugh. Jacinta always made him laugh with all her prim little rules and guidelines. In public, that was. In private she was as dirty as the next woman—if the next woman had a penchant for hard, sweaty sex. They'd been friends for years now, lovers when the mood took them. When he'd built his new house near the St. Kilda shore six months ago, she'd volunteered to help him decorate it. The catch had been that she wanted to redecorate him—"civilize him," as she put it—at the same time.

"I don't know why you're so resistant to the idea of stepping it up a notch," Jacinta said. "If you had any idea how good you look in a suit, you wouldn't think twice."

"I'm a bike builder. I spend my days covered in grease," he said.

"You're a millionaire. You never have to get your hands dirty again if you don't want to."

"Babe, you have your world, I have mine. I'm not going to ask you to bend metal for me. And you're not going to get me in a tie."

She looked as though she was going to argue some more, then she shrugged. "Stubborn bastard. Come on, I'll show you the pieces I've picked out for you," she said, taking his hand and guiding him into the gallery itself.

A few heads turned as they walked the length of the space past asymmetrical sculptures and brightly hued canvases and jagged twists of metal. Five years ago Liam would have figured people were looking at him because he so clearly didn't belong. His hair was too long, his walk had too much swagger to it, his hands were too rough and ready. Back then, he'd have stared every person down, maybe taken his attitude right up to a few of them to show them how much he didn't care for their opinion of him. Now he ignored them because he knew he didn't have to prove anything to anyone, ever. He had the big house, the big car and the big bank account to prove it.

Jacinta stopped in front of a smooth obelisk of shiny white stone.

"I thought this would be nice on the balcony in the west corner," she said.

He eyed it for a long beat, not saying a word. Jacinta slanted a look at him.

"You don't like it, do you?"

"No," he said. "It looks like a big stone dildo. Call me crazy, but no man wants something that big casting a shadow over his life."

She sighed. "For a man who doesn't know much about art, you certainly have strong opinions."

"I want to see some craftsmanship, that's all. Any of the fabricators at my workshop could make this before lunch," he said.

"Lovely. Maybe we should ask them to whip up a few for us, then," Jacinta said dryly.

He shrugged, unapologetic. She narrowed her eyes in thought for a moment then nodded decisively.

"Follow me. We've got a smaller collection in one of the side spaces. I have a feeling Paulo Gregorio's work might be more up your alley," she said.

Liam followed her across the polished concrete floor, admiring the sway of her hips. He wondered if she was wearing garters and stockings like she had been the last time she stayed the night. He loved a woman in red lace—it was one weakness he was more than happy to admit to.

"Okay, this artist is definitely more traditional. I think you'll find all the craftsmanship you could possibly want in his work," Jacinta said as they stepped into a smaller room.

Eight large canvases hung on the four walls. They were all portraits, all women in various stages of undress. Jacinta pointed to the first painting, a six-foot-by-six-foot canvas of a woman lying on a chaise lounge, a filmy negligee falling off her shoulders and tangling in her legs.

"Lots of color. Strong technique. And a subject that I know is very close to your heart," Jacinta said.

He smiled at her dry humor as he studied the painting, noting the warm look in the woman's eyes, the delicate way the artist had captured the texture of her clothing and the blush on her skin.

"Nice work," he said.

"Nice work? It's not one of your motorbikes, Liam."

He checked the price list in her hand.

"You're right. A custom Masters Mechanics bike is worth three times as much."

She rolled her eyes. "What about this next one? I was thinking it would look great in your bathroom, above that huge Roman tub."

Liam dutifully shifted his attention from the lounging woman to the next painting. This canvas was bigger, eight-by-ten, he estimated, and the subject was completely naked, lying sprawled on her back on a forest-green quilt. Her arms were spread wide and one knee was bent, the leg dropping out to the side. He followed the line of her calves to her thighs and the mysterious shadows between them. The artist had only hinted at what a man would be able to see in real life, but it was enough. More than enough.

If he had this painting in his bathroom, he'd be taking a cold shower every freaking day.

"I don't suppose the artist hands out phone numbers with each painting?" he asked, only half joking.

Jacinta made an impatient noise. "Does that mean you like it?"

He dragged his gaze from the plump tips of the woman's breasts and shifted his attention to her face.

Then he forgot to breathe.

Took a step backward.

Made a noise in the back of his throat that may or may not have been a four-letter word.

Green eyes. A dimpled chin. Long dark hair.

A face he remembered in his dreams. The most bitter-sweet memory of his life.

Zoe.

"Damn."

Jacinta touched his arm. "Liam. What's wrong?"

His gaze swept the painting again, looking for proof that he was wrong. Again he saw those open thighs, her hips, her breasts. And Zoe's face. Indisputably Zoe's face.

He stepped forward.

Why would she do this? Put herself on display like this? Little Zoe, spread across the wall for any man to stare at.

"Liam! What are you doing?" Jacinta demanded as he gripped the sides of the painting.

"Who else has seen this? How long has it been on display?" he asked.

"Liam, put that back. My God, what is wrong with you?"

He lifted the painting off its hook and turned it around. Only when it was leaning against the wall, face in, did he relax.

"Wrap it up. I don't want anyone else looking at it."

Jacinta planted both hands on her hips and glared at him.

"Would you mind putting the painting back, please?"

He pulled his checkbook out. "How much is it? I'm taking it with me."

Jacinta stared at him for a long moment.

"You're serious, aren't you?"

He waited for her to name the price.

"It's fifteen thousand," she finally said.

He wrote the check and tore it off. "I want to speak to this Paulo guy. Tonight."

"Look, I don't know what's going on, but—"

"I know her," he said bluntly. "Or at least I used to know her. I don't know what this guy offered her to sit for this painting, but she doesn't belong up here."

"For God's sake, Liam, you sound like an outraged parent. This is art, not pornography."

"Can you get me this guy's number or not?"

Jacinta studied him, frowning.

"I don't want you calling one of my artists and harassing him. What do you want to know? Her contact details, I suppose?"

"For starters."

"Give me five minutes."

Jacinta disappeared toward the rear of the gallery where he knew she had her office. Once he was alone he ran a hand through his hair and closed his eyes. He felt sick. Like someone had punched him in the guts.

This Paulo shithead must have offered her big money to pose for him. She must have been so desperate it seemed like a good deal. Damn, what the hell was Tom doing, letting his little sister get into this kind of trouble?

The tap of heels heralded Jacinta's return. She handed over a scrap of paper.

"No home number, just her workplace. She's very private, according to Paulo."

He studied the address and phone number. The Blue Rose, on the western side of the city in Footscray. Not exactly the most up-and-coming area. He wondered what kind of business it was.

"Can you get someone to wrap the painting?" he asked.

"I don't suppose there's any point in asking if you would

mind leaving it until the show is finished so I don't have a dirty great gap in my display?" Jacinta countered.

"No."

She sighed. "I didn't think so."

She headed off again, but stopped in the doorway.

"By the way, I asked what he paid her to sit for him."

"And?"

"It was a freebie. No fee."

He shook his head. He refused to believe it.

"No way."

Jacinta simply raised her eyebrows before swiveling on her heel and continuing out the door.

Forty minutes later he pulled up in front of the address he'd been given. He leaned forward over the steering wheel to check the number above the shop door was correct.

The Blue Rose was a tattoo parlor.

It was the last thing he'd expected. He stared at the dingy front window for a long time before he threw his black SUV into gear and drove home. All the way, he thought about the Fords, felt again the mix of guilt and regret and gratitude that he always experienced when he remembered their kindness to him. Wondered where he would have wound up if it hadn't been for them taking him in. In a state home, most probably. A problem teen no one wanted to take on.

But the Fords had. They'd supported him through his mom's brief but brutal illness, then they'd asked him to live with them, offering him their backyard studio. They'd even renovated it for him—new paint, new carpet, insulation so he wouldn't stew in his own juices in summer.

He and Tom had been best mates, a friendship that hadn't come easily to Liam. He and his mom had been on the road, moving around for so long that he'd stopped bothering to make friends. He'd seen so much ugliness that it was hard for him to invest in the same things that other kids his age were into—music, cars, chicks. But Tom had made it easy, as had his family. And Zoe…

He could still remember the first time he'd seen her. Tom had brought Liam home after school, and they'd been standing at the open fridge door, drinking soda straight from the bottle when she came into the room. She'd been wearing a pair of cutoff denim shorts and a tank top, her dark, straight hair in a ponytail. Her legs were long and slim, but she seemed uncertain of them, like a baby giraffe trying to walk for the first time. The buds of her breasts pressed against her top, ripe and full of potential. And those eyes…those incredible green eyes.

He'd taken one look at her and choked on the mouthful of soda he'd been swallowing.

She was special. He'd known it the moment he saw her. Every second he spent with her afterward only confirmed it. Over the past twelve years, he'd wondered how she was, what she'd become. She'd be twenty-seven now. He'd always assumed she'd be married, maybe with kids of her own.

He dumped the painting in his empty dining room when he got home. He leaned it against the wall and stared at Zoe's exposed body, the image blurred by bubble wrap.

This was not something he'd ever imagined for her.

He turned away. He wanted to look at her again, to tear off the bubble wrap and feast on her. Which was exactly why he wasn't going to. He closed his eyes and forced himself to remember her laugh, the trust in her eyes when she used to look at him, the utter honesty and vulnerability in her face and body when she'd told him she loved him.

Zoe Ford deserved better than this painting and that tattoo shop. First thing tomorrow he was going to seek her out and do whatever it took to put things right in her world.

"HEY, HOW ARE WE this beautiful morning?" Zoe asked as she pushed through the back door into the Blue Rose's workroom.

"Zoe! Man, I was starting to sweat about you," Jake Lewis said, throwing her a frustrated look.

She made a big show of checking her watch.

"I'm right on time for my ten-thirty appointment, Jake," she told her boss.

"Would it kill you to get here twenty minutes earlier?"

"You know I don't need the prep time. It's all up here, baby," she said, tapping a forefinger against her temple.

She shrugged out of her denim jacket and threw it on a chair. Her cowboy boots thumped solidly on the concrete floor as she crossed to her workbench and began setting up for her client.

"Anyone ever told you you're a smart-ass, Ford?"

"Oh, yeah. First time today, though, so you get a prize." She flipped her middle finger at him. As she'd hoped, he laughed.

She smoothed her hands down her lace-up jeans as she considered her workbench. Everything looked good—disposable ink cups, new needles ready to go.

"You still performing tonight?" Jake asked as she crossed to the autoclave to collect her sterilized gun.

"Nine o'clock. You going to be there? I'll put your name on the door."

"Don't know if my blood pressure can take it."

She rolled her eyes. "Pussy."

Jake moved to the front of the shop and she tugged off the long-sleeved T-shirt she was wearing over a snug black tank. She always got warm when she worked, and she wasn't about to stop in the middle of inking someone's back to shrug off her clothes.

She heard the front bell sound and checked the clock. Her

client was on time. She raised an eyebrow; she'd lost the bet she'd made with herself. This client had been so nervous when they discussed his appointment that she'd been sure he'd be a no-show, or as they called them, a B-back—the kind of customer who made some excuse to slip out just before the needle touched his skin, promising he'd "be back" but in reality never to be seen again.

She heard the low rumble of a man's voice as she bagged her spray bottles to prevent cross-contamination.

"Sure, whatever, go through. She's in the back," she heard Jake say.

Heavy footsteps sounded on the floor as her customer approached. For some reason her stomach tightened and a shiver of something raced up her spine. Excitement? Fear? Premonition?

She had her back to the door when a deep male voice spoke.

"Zoe?"

All the little hairs stood up on the back of her neck. Slowly she turned around to confirm what her ears were telling her.

Liam. Standing there larger than life, bigger and taller than any of her memories of him. Her chest felt as though someone was sitting on it as she took in the messy dark hair brushing the collar of his leather jacket, the deep brown of his eyes, the crooked line of his nose. His jaw was still strong and stubborn-looking, his shoulders still wide. Some things had changed. His chest was deeper and broader than when he'd been seventeen, making his hips seem narrower, and his thighs were more muscled and bulky. The boy had become a man. A big, powerful man.

Of all the tattoo parlors in Melbourne, she couldn't believe he had walked into hers. What were the odds?

Hard on the heels of shock at seeing him came a searing

wash of anger. Twelve years of resentment and bitterness welled up inside her. The way he'd thrown what she offered him in her face. The way he'd left without a word. And what had happened afterward when she was too wild with grief at losing him to care about anything, especially herself.

"Masters," she said, crossing her arms over her breasts. She was proud of how cool and unsurprised her voice sounded. "This is a surprise. Long time no see."

He stared at her and she could see the shock and disbelief in his eyes as he surveyed her from head to toe, taking in her skintight jeans and tank, her breasts spilling over her neckline, the dark kohl on her eyes, the deep red on her lips.

"Jesus, Zoe," he said. "What the hell are you doing here?"

He was surprised by the grown-up her—that much was obvious.

"What does it look like? I work here. If you're after some ink, I've got an appointment right now. You'll have to come back later."

His gaze took in her workbench, the scuffed concrete floor, the curling corners on the many sheets of tattoo flash art stuck to the walls.

"Does Tom know about all this?" he asked.

He sounded grim. Disapproving.

"Excuse me?"

He ran a hand through his hair, a gesture she remembered from all those years ago.

"You don't belong here," he said.

She straightened, planted her hands on her hips. "Don't I? What would you know, Liam? What the hell would you know about me?"

His gaze dropped to her breasts, then just as quickly came back to her face.

"I bought a painting last night. By Paulo Gregorio."

She stared at him for a long beat. Then she laughed. He hadn't just walked in off the street and coincidentally found her. He'd come looking for her.

"I get it. You bought Paulo's painting and you decided to look me up. What's wrong, Liam? Did you suddenly realize what you missed out on all those years ago?"

He frowned. "I wanted to find out what had gone wrong."

Her chin came up and her eyes narrowed. "Wrong?"

"That you needed to do something like that."

She shook her head, truly staggered by his arrogance.

"Wow. Haven't you become the morals campaigner. Let me save you the bother of worrying about me. I'm fine. In fact, I'm better than fine. I'm exactly where I want to be."

"I don't believe that."

She laughed again, a sound totally without humor. "I don't give a damn what you believe or don't believe. Who the hell do you think you are, walking into my life and telling me I'm wrong and looking at me as though I just offered you a blow job for a tenner?"

"I was worried about you," he said.

She swore and stared at the ceiling as she struggled to keep a grip on her temper. Her lips curled into a sneer when she looked at him again.

"Twelve years too late, baby," she said. "Now, how about you get the hell out of my space?"

He stared at her.

"Go! I don't want to see you or speak to you," she said. To her great shame, hot tears burned at the back of her eyes. She held them there by sheer dint of will as they eyeballed each other.

"Fine. But this isn't over," he said.

She swore again, telling him exactly what she thought of him and where he could go, with bells on.

He gave her one last, long look before turning on his heel

and exiting. She reached for the countertop behind her and grasped the edge to stop her rubbery knees from collapsing. Then a more urgent need gripped her. One hand pressed to her mouth, she just made it to the restroom before she lost her breakfast to the toilet bowl.

How she hated him. How she hated herself for still feeling anything for him after all these years.

She ducked her head over the sink and rinsed her mouth out. Her eyes were guarded as she surveyed herself in the chipped mirror above the sink.

For the first time in a long time, she felt a stab of the phantom pain that had haunted her for so long after the operation. She pressed a hand to her belly.

A knock sounded on the bathroom door.

"You in here, Zoe? Your tenderfoot's arrived for his ten-thirty appointment," Jake called.

"I'll be out in a minute," she said.

She rinsed her mouth again, then pressed her cool, wet hands against her cheeks.

Screw Liam Masters. She didn't give a damn about him or what he thought of her. She exited the bathroom and put on her brightest, sassiest smile for the scared teenager standing uncertainly in the doorway of her workroom.

"Rodney. Great to see you. Let's turn you into a piece of walking, talking art, baby," she said.

LIAM THOUGHT ABOUT ZOE all day at work. He thought about the look in her eyes when she'd first seen him and recognized him. He thought about her attitude, all sharp edges and defenses. He thought about the length of her legs and the fullness of her breasts, every detail of both on display thanks to her painted-on clothes. He thought about the tattoo on her neck, a striking overblown rose in shades of black and gray.

Zoe. His Zoe, all grown up. And nothing like he'd ever imagined her. Certainly not happily married with kids.

He couldn't reconcile the woman he'd met today with the girl he'd known twelve years ago. It didn't seem possible that the pure, innocent, generous spirit that had been Zoe could grow up into a woman so hard and edgy.

He couldn't afford to be this distracted right now. The workshop was operating at full capacity, and as always, there were fires to put out. Delays on the parts they'd ordered for a custom chopper that had a strict delivery date. Problems with the fit of the double-overhead engine one client had requested.

He discussed options and solutions with his chief designer and lead fabricator, Vinnie. He wrangled suppliers. He put a rocket up one of the assembly teams to ensure they kept to schedule. At a quarter to seven, he shrugged into his leather jacket and headed for the door.

"Where are you going?" Vinnie asked in surprise. It was a rare day when Liam wasn't the last one to leave the workshop.

"There's something I have to do."

"I need to talk to you about this biker build-off comp. You still want to enter?"

Vinnie sounded doubtful. Liam gave him a cuff on the shoulder.

"I know it'll be a pain in the ass, but we have to keep pushing the PR."

Vinnie's disgust showed on his face. "What a load of BS. Why can't we just make great bikes like we always have? That's how we got to where we are today."

"Don't you listen to the marketing eggheads? We're building a brand now, my friend," Liam said on his way out the door. "I'll sort out our entry first thing tomorrow. Make sure you reserve time in the production schedule so we can give it our best."

He palmed his car keys as he crossed the parking lot. Masters Mechanics had taken on a life of its own over the past three years. Through word of mouth they'd doubled, then tripled in size. Turnover was in the millions. He had more than thirty staff working for him, including a marketing manager. The days of simply shutting himself in the workshop and bending metal until it looked good to him were over. He had responsibilities, commitments. And— even though it had always felt like a dirty word, given his background—ambitions. Not world domination, but definitely he wanted Masters Mechanics to be the go-to shop for custom motorbikes across Australia and New Zealand. Definitely.

The V8 engine of his vintage Mustang burbled to life as he turned the key in the ignition. He took the tollway across town to save time and was pulling up in front of the Blue Rose at a quarter to eight. The lights shone inside and he could see Zoe talking to a couple of customers at the front counter. Good. She hadn't gone home. He'd taken note of the parlor's opening hours when she'd kicked him out and taken a punt that she'd be working till close at eight. If she hadn't been here, he would have simply come back another time.

He watched her for a moment, the way she propped her hip against the counter, the way she tilted her head back and shook it to draw her hair away from her face. He'd wait until the customers left then go in to talk to her again. Try to keep things calmer this time, not get her back up. He winced every time he remembered asking her what had gone wrong. Zoe had always been proud. No surprise that she'd cut up at him.

But he needed to let her know that if she needed help, he was there to give it. It was the least he owed her and her family.

He smiled humorlessly. Yeah, he was a real freaking saint. Pity he couldn't stop himself from thinking about that painting, about those shadows between her thighs, about the wealth of breast spilling over the top of her tank top even now as she leaned an elbow on the counter and sketched a design on a piece of paper. Her two potential clients were no doubt copping a decent eyeful. Probably thought all their Christmases had come at once. He gripped the steering wheel, his knuckles white.

It was nearly eight when the two men exited the parlor. He watched them break into laughter the moment they were outside, slapping each other on the back. One of them looked back over his shoulder at Zoe, and Liam knew without a doubt that they were talking about her, about what they'd like to do to her if they were lucky enough to get her naked.

The car door was open before he could think twice. He crossed the road, hands curled into fists. At close quarters, he could see they were young, barely old enough to drive. He stopped in his tracks and let them walk away, still laughing. He forced his hands to relax.

He'd almost lost it there for a minute. What the hell was wrong with him?

He took a deep, rib-expanding breath, then let it out slowly. He prided himself on the fact that it had been many, many years since he'd thrown a punch in anger. For a bunch of other reasons, sure, but never because impulse urged him to. It was one of the abiding tenets of his life—never lose control. That, and his determination to remain single.

He turned his focus back to the tattoo parlor and strode to the front door. He frowned when the handle refused to give beneath his hand. Shit. She'd shut up for the night while he was wasting time on the sidewalk. His guess was confirmed as the lights were switched off.

Fine. He'd come back tomorrow. He made his way back to his car and was about to pull away from the curb when a seen-better-days Subaru WRX drove past, Zoe behind the wheel.

He fell in behind her automatically. He already knew she had an unlisted telephone number and address. At least if he followed her home, he'd know where she lived.

2

LIAM TRAILED ZOE through the night-dark city for twenty minutes until they were driving through the graffiti-covered streets of North Melbourne. He almost gave himself away by braking sharply when she pulled over to the curb without indicating. He pulled over when he found a parking spot half a block up. He twisted in his seat to watch as she exited her car.

She was carrying a gym bag and walking with purpose, her long legs eating up the sidewalk as she approached the front door to a nightclub.

Not going home, then. He watched the entrance for five minutes, but she didn't come out. He shrugged and exited his car. He'd talk to her in there. The venue didn't matter, what he had to say—and offer—did.

He locked the Mustang and walked toward the club. A big guy in a tight black T-shirt blocked the entrance, arms crossed over his chest. Liam glanced at the club name—Thrashed—before eyeing the bouncer in front of him. The guy eyed him back for a long beat before moving aside. Liam passed through into a small foyer. Loud music leaked out from the club proper and he paid a ten-dollar cover charge to the guy behind the counter.

He pushed through double swing doors to find himself in a dimly lit space dotted with tables and chairs, one wall all bar, the opposite wall a stage. It was early and there were only a handful of people at the tables. Zoe wasn't one of them.

He scanned the bar, but she wasn't there, either. Where the hell was she? He waited ten minutes to see if she'd gone to the bathroom, then walked outside to make sure her car was still in the street. It was.

He returned to the club and bought a beer. Over the next twenty minutes, the club slowly filled. And still Zoe hadn't appeared. The loud music was getting on his nerves by then and he decided to call it quits and look Zoe up again tomorrow. After all, she'd survived twelve years without him. She'd survive one more night.

He was shouldering his way to the exit when the lights flashed and the audience began to clap and whistle. The room dimmed and the stage lights came up as a band sauntered onto the stage: a drummer with long stringy hair and too many piercings; a bass guitarist with big biceps and the crookedest nose Liam had ever seen; and a lead guitarist in tight leather with a bare chest. His guitar slung across his shoulder, the lead guitarist leaned in toward the mike stand.

"Yo! We're Sugar Cane and you know what you got to do, people. Tell Vixen how much you want her!" he hollered.

The crowd went nuts. Screaming, whistling, stomping their feet. Liam turned toward the exit, glad to be leaving before his eardrums started bleeding.

"Relax, boys and girls. Vixen is more than ready to come out and play," a sultry female voice said.

Liam turned to the stage, instinct telling him he wasn't going to like what he was about to see. The crowd took it up a notch, screaming and stomping as a woman strutted onto the stage in black, four-inch stilettos. She wore black fishnet stockings with red satin garters and a pair of tiny black patent leather hot pants. A strip of belly and most of her breasts were bared by a tight black leather vest. Her face was painted white like a geisha and her eyes burned out at the audience from a band of black makeup that striped the upper part of her face like a mask. Her lips jumped out in brilliant red, a match for the single vibrant streak running through her rock-and-roll hair.

He stood stock-still, staring at Zoe as she slowly rotated her hips in a suggestive circle.

"Let's hit it, lovers!" she howled into the mike, and loud, pumping thrash blew out at him from the speaker stack.

Zoe started to sing, her voice strong and sultry as she strutted across the small stage. She pumped her arm in the air, thrust her hips. She slid a hand over her crotch and threw her head back in feigned ecstasy as she sang about sex and desire and taking what she wanted when she wanted it.

He stood frozen at the exit for almost the entire first song. Finally he shouldered his way back through the crowd to take up a position against the bar, his arms folded across his chest as he watched Zoe perform.

He'd never seen anything like her. Without a doubt, every heterosexual man in the place was hard. Probably half the gay ones, too. She was every man's darkest fantasy: pure, unbridled sex, strutting, shaking it, daring every man in the audience to want her, to try to satisfy her.

Halfway through the second song, she tugged at the studs on her vest and pulled it open to reveal a black lace bra and a second rose tattoo across her hip and half her belly. The crowd howled its approval. She slid a hand from one breast to the other then down her stomach, all the while singing about liking it hard and fast. She turned her back as she threw the vest to one side. He stared as the rest of her tattoo was revealed.

Etched into her skin in shades of black and gray, the tattoo curved around her hip to climb her spine, a thorny rambling rose that promised as much pleasure as it did pain. It disappeared beneath the tangle of her hair only to reappear again as it twined its way around her throat.

Movement near the front of the stage drew his attention. A bare-chested, burly skinhead was hauling himself over the lip of the stage. Liam started pushing his way through the crowd, seeing the inevitable in his mind's eye—some drunken idiot pawing at Zoe, security rushing in, fists being thrown, broken faces and bones. He'd barely taken three steps before Zoe walked straight up to the interloper and placed the spike of her heel dead center of his chest. She didn't drop a note as she pushed him off the stage.

Liam stopped, staring at her for a long moment.

He had no idea who she was, what had made her into the woman onstage whipping four-hundred-odd people into a sweaty, horny frenzy.

Slowly he returned to his station at the bar.

It was going to be a long night.

SWEAT TRICKLED DOWN Zoe's spine as she worked the stage. For the first time all day, she felt like herself. Seeing Liam Masters again after so long had thrown her, dredged up some of the bad, old stuff from the past. But she'd burned it off by the time she sang the chorus to "Come and Get Me," and by the time she was on her knees belting out "Release Me," she felt invincible.

Mikey hammered out the last few chords of the song as she pounded her fists into the stage, thrashing her hair around. She was grinning like a madwoman when she stood and made her way to the drum riser to grab the bottle of water she'd dumped there, the thunder of applause vibrating through the soles of her stilettos.

"You are on fire tonight, babe," Kane, the drummer, said as she dropped her head back and sucked down water.

"I feel good," she said. "What's next?"

"'Make It Hurt,'" Kane said, checking the playlist taped to the floor beside his kit.

Zoe lifted the hair off the back of her neck.

"Okay, let's go."

She strode to the front of the stage to grab the mike. Faces screamed up at her out of the audience. She loved these gigs. Becoming Vixen for the night was about the most fun she could have without being naked or partaking of prohibited substances. The opening riff of "Make It Hurt" roared out of the speakers. She planted her feet wide and pushed her hips forward as she ground out the lyrics. She stared out into the darkness of the club. All she could see was a sea of black, but occasionally individual faces were picked out by the roaming spot. Dancing women dressed like herself, in as little as possible. Built men shaking their fists in the air. Bright-pink hair, neon blue.

Her stomach flipped when the spotlight roamed across the bar and she caught a flash of a tall man standing there, arms crossed over his chest, his gaze drilling into her. Just a flash, but her body told her who it was.

Liam, here.

Watching her.

Her first reaction was anger that he'd invaded yet more of her territory. Then she remembered the way he'd eyed her this morning, as though he couldn't quite believe his eyes, and her sense of humor came to the rescue. If he hadn't approved of the tattoo parlor and her tight jeans, she could only imagine what he was thinking right now.

The thought was so delicious she had trouble not laughing into the mike.

Knowing he was watching added new spice to every move she made, every word she sang. When she slid a hand from breast to breast and arched her back, she made sure he got an uninterrupted full-frontal view. When she offered her backside to the audience and slowly swiveled her hips, she imagined him watching, grinding his teeth over how *wrong* it all was.

She felt high, all powerful, dizzy with the danger of it. She could feel him brooding out in the audience, could sense his heavy disapproval beating at her from across the room. And she didn't care. She so didn't care.

By the time she belted out the last song, she was buzzing with adrenaline. She took her bow with the rest of the band, but her eyes sought Liam in the darkness. She could just make out his silhouette and she threw him a cocky, knowing smile before turning on her heel and striding offstage, working her hips and ass for all they were worth.

Take that, asshole.

"Man, what a gig! Best night in ages!" Derek, Sugar Cane's bass player, said as they made their way down the stairs to the change rooms.

"Zoe, baby, you rocked hard tonight," her lead guitarist, Mikey, said. "I thought we were gonna have to beat the audience off with a stick."

"You guys were great," Zoe told them. "I had a good time."

Kane grabbed a six-pack of beer from the fridge in the band room and offered them around. Zoe shook her head, reaching instead for the bottle of bourbon she'd opened before the show.

"We heard anything more about those gigs up in Sydney?" she asked as she took a pull straight from the bottle.

"Nah. I'll get onto the promoter tomorrow, chase him down. You know what those guys are like," Derek said.

The guys collapsed onto the saggy, stained couch in the corner. Zoe propped her butt on a table and lifted her hair off the back of her neck.

"Man, I am steaming," she said. She could feel sweat rolling down between her breasts.

"You said it, baby." Mikey's gaze was fixed on her legs.

No prizes for guessing what he wanted. But Zoe wasn't in the mood for Mikey tonight. He got way too possessive after sex and it messed with the band dynamic too much. She wasn't any man's property.

"I'm going to go clean up," she said.

She hooked the neck of the bourbon bottle between two fingers and made her way down the cinder-block corridor to the pokey change room. Inside, her work clothes were draped over the back of a chair, and her makeup kit was folded open on the counter in front of the mirror. She took another pull from the bottle and eyed herself in the mirror. A smile tugged at the corners of her mouth as she again imagined Liam Masters's reaction to Vixen's performance.

Hilarious. Way, way too funny.

Then she heard the scuff of footsteps and turned her head to see him filling the doorway—tall and dark and intense.

Her smile widened into a grin and she raised the bourbon bottle in salute to him.

"How'd you like the show?" She held up a finger before he had a chance to speak. "No, no, let me guess. You thought it was all wrong."

He didn't say a word, just walked into the room and pushed the door shut behind him.

Suddenly the small space seemed even smaller. Zoe took another mouthful of bourbon.

"We need to talk," Liam said.

"Do we?"

"I want to help you out. If you need money, a fresh start. Whatever. I'll get you whatever you need," he said.

She slowly put down the bottle. He was offering her charity. Like she was some down-and-out junkie or streetwalker.

"Gee, thanks, Lord Liam. How good of you to come down amongst the peasants and offer your bounty. I feel so privileged, I hardly know what to say."

His gaze swept her from head to toe.

"Do your parents know you do this kind of thing? Your brother?"

She was a little sick of the judgment in his tone.

"This kind of thing? What exactly are you referring to, Liam? My singing? My career?"

"I'm talking about putting yourself on display for anyone to look at," he said. "Letting every man and his dog stare at you and imagine what it would be like to screw you stupid."

She shrugged, knowing somehow that it was the one reaction that would really piss him off.

"Men can look and imagine all they want. I'm the one who decides when and what they can touch."

She raised her chin, daring him to say more. The silence stretched between them for what felt like a long time.

"What happened to you, Zoe?" he finally asked, his voice low.

She blinked, caught off guard by the pain in his face, the sincerity in his tone.

"You left and I grew up," she said, turning her back on him. She didn't trust herself to look him in the eye.

She could feel him watching her as she stowed her cosmetics in her kit.

"Let me help you. For old times' sake."

She closed her eyes, despising herself for the way he could still make her feel. Tears threatened for the second time that day and the emptiness inside her yawned wide.

God, she had to get him out of her change room and out of her life.

It had taken her years to find a place and a persona that made it all bearable, doable, survivable. She would not let him strip her of her armor.

She let her eyelids drop over her eyes as she turned to face him, at the same time hooking one thumb into the waistband of her hot pants.

"I don't need any help from you, Liam," she said. "The only thing I need from any man is the one thing I don't have myself. If you get my drift."

She watched as her meaning dawned on him and his expression grew even grimmer.

If that didn't get rid of her self-appointed Sir Galahad, she didn't know what would. After all, it had worked a treat twelve years ago.

"Don't play games," he said. "There must be something you need."

"Definitely," she said. "Especially after performing. It always makes me hot."

She fanned a hand in front of her face. At the same time, she used the thumb in her waistband to pop the stud on her hot pants. The small sound brought Liam's gaze to her waist.

"Not interested?" she asked, finding the tab of her zipper with her fingertips.

She had a sudden flash of how it had been all those years ago, the way he'd slid his hand under the waistband of her jeans at first rather than undo her fly, how she'd had to beg him to touch her properly.

The memory urged her on as she slid her zipper down.

"Don't." His voice sounded too loud in the small space.

A muscle jumped in his jaw.

Good. She wanted him to sweat. She wanted him gone.

And she was enjoying being the one with the power for a change. Once, she'd begged him to love her and he'd pushed her out the door, then abandoned her without a word. Tonight, she was the one in charge.

She snagged her thumbs into the belt loops of her hot pants and pushed down. She had to wriggle her hips a little to get the leather over them.

"Tight," she said, wrinkling her nose. She pushed the hot pants down her legs and stepped out of them, standing in front of him wearing only her black lace thong and bra and her red garters and stockings.

"So what's it going to be, Liam? Are you going to give me what I need, or are you going to make me take care of things myself?"

She touched the tip of her middle finger to her tongue then slid her finger down her chest until she found her left nipple through the lace of her bra. She brushed it lightly, then caught it between thumb and forefinger and squeezed. Heat shot down her belly to her thighs and her nipple hardened into a tight, needy peak.

She could hear him breathing.

"I just want to make things right for you," he said.

"And I told you how you could do that."

She'd meant to drive him away, but the way he was watching her so intently was having its own effect on her. Suddenly it wasn't a game anymore.

She'd always imagined what it would be like to be with him. She'd held him in her hands, stroked him, found the single bead of desire that had glistened on the head of his penis. She'd had his fingers between her legs, inside her. She'd been so desperate for him that she'd begged him to take her virginity. But he'd pushed her away and left her wanting.

Not this time. Not if she had any say in the matter. She took a step backward until she felt the cool ridge of the counter against the backs of her thighs. She propped her butt against it and lifted her leg up onto the seat of the chair beside it.

She held his eye all the while, watching him watching her.

He wanted her. The tension in his body would have betrayed him even if there hadn't been a bigger, longer giveaway bulging the front of his well-worn jeans.

"What's wrong, Liam? I'm not Tom's innocent little sister anymore. No parents are going to come barging in. It's just you and me. No excuses, nothing."

She kept her left hand on her breast and slid her right down her belly until she felt the lace of her thong beneath her fingers. She slid her fingers beneath the elastic and between her thighs.

Between taunting him so publicly onstage and this far more private, provocative session, she was aching for fulfillment.

She closed her eyes and sucked in a breath as she circled her finger.

"Feels so good, Liam. Want to try?"

LIAM SWORE. He was so hard it hurt and he was about out of reasons for keeping his hands off her. She was touching herself, her hips circling as she pleasured herself right in front of him. He couldn't remember ever being so confronted, turned-on and conflicted all at the same time.

But this was Zoe. Zoe of the big trusting eyes and the silken, untouched skin and the breathless, utterly guileless sexuality. He couldn't screw her in the back room of some shitty club.

"Better hurry up, Liam, or the show will be over." She pushed down the cup of her bra and exposed one full, creamy breast.

All night he'd watched her, wondering, remembering. He wasn't made of stone, and he wasn't a saint.

He crossed the space between them in two strides. Her eyes widened as he grabbed her shoulders.

Then he was kissing her, forcing her head back as he thrust his tongue into her mouth. Her hands found his shoulders as his whole body crashed into hers, his chest meeting her breasts, his hips pressing into her widespread thighs.

He was so hungry for her he didn't know where to start. He shoved her bra straps off her shoulders and pushed the cups down to bare both her breasts. She sucked in a shuddering breath as he slid his hands over her. He kissed her neck, tasting the salt of sweat and the tang of her perfume. He stuck his tongue in her ear and pinched her nipples firmly, making her squirm against him.

She was panting, her eyes closed, her hands clutching his backside as she dragged him closer. He rubbed himself against her as he slid a hand down her belly. His fingers found her through the thin lace of her thong, gliding into damp heat. He pushed the lace to one side and felt the smooth slide of his fingers on slick, hairless skin.

Zoe waxed.

Of course she did.

She felt swollen and juicy against his fingers, so slippery and hot he couldn't wait another second. She was ahead of him, her hands dragging at the stud on his jeans, pulling his fly down. He groaned low in the back of his throat as she stroked a knowing hand up and down his shaft. He pressed forward, wanting inside her. His whole body tensed as the sensitive head of his erection encountered her slick heat.

"Wait," she said, her voice a low husk.

He heard the crinkle of foil, then she was sliding protection onto him with expert hands. No sooner had she smoothed the latex to the base of his shaft than he was thrusting forward. Tight heat engulfed him. She let out a surprised moan as he gave her his all. Then he lost all sense of place and time as he pounded into her.

Her legs came up to lock around his waist. Her head dropped back on her neck. Her body shuddered with the impact of each stroke and she caught her bottom lip between her teeth to stifle a cry. He leaned forward and pulled a nipple into his mouth, stroking her with his tongue even as he stroked her with his cock. He bit her, savoring the jerk of her hips and the tight throb of her inner muscles around him.

Again and again he drove into her until he had to slide his hands onto her butt so he could go deeper, harder. Her back arched and her fingernails dug into his backside. Her mouth fell open as she shuddered around him, a look of pleasurable pain contorting her face as she came and came. Then his own orgasm hit him like a fist, driving the air from his lungs as he ground himself into her. For long seconds he shuddered out his release, every muscle hard as steel.

Then he was still inside her but the urgency was gone. He could feel her breath against his neck, her hands gripping his butt. A trickle of sweat ran down his side. He registered the distant, muffled sound of music from the club.

His heart was thundering in his chest. He took a deep breath, trying to regain some semblance of control.

Because he'd just lost it, big-time.

Zoe's body began to tremble against his and he drew back so he could look into her face. She was laughing silently, shaking her head from side to side.

"I guess I should thank you," she said. "You said I would, one day. It might just have been worth waiting twelve years, after all."

He slid free from her and turned away to take care of the condom, wrapping it and throwing it in the waste bin. The small piece of business gave him an excuse not to look at her.

There was something so desolate in her eyes, so empty and sad that it made him want to punch something.

He slid his zipper closed and buttoned his jeans. Zoe pulled her bra back up, then started to unclip her stockings from her red garters.

"I didn't mean for this to happen," he said.

"Neither did I, believe it or not. But it turned out to be a pretty good idea, don't you think?"

She rolled her stockings down her legs and toed off her stilettos.

He looked away when she slid her thong down, forcing his gaze from the narrow strip of hair between her thighs. She was bare between them, he knew now. Smooth and so damned hot she'd blown his mind.

She stepped into a clean pair of panties then reached for her jeans.

"Can we go somewhere? To talk?" he asked as she dragged them on and tightened the leather laces that held them closed.

"I told you, I don't want or need your help, Liam. You just gave me all I'll ever want from you."

Her gaze was steady as she pulled on her tank top.

She meant it. Which left him with nowhere to go, nothing to offer.

"How long have you been singing?" he asked. Mostly because he figured it was a neutral question and he needed to buy time to get his head together.

"Five years now. Three years as Vixen. She makes it a lot more fun."

She moved to stand in front of the mirror, reaching for a tub of face cream. Her gaze found his in the mirror.

"What about you, Mr. Do-Gooder. What do you do for a crust?"

"I build custom motorbikes. Mostly choppers."

She pulled her hair into a ponytail and smoothed cream over her face, closing her eyes as she cleansed her eye makeup.

"Figures. You were always fiddling in the garage, tinkering with something or other."

She wiped her face with a tissue. Pink skin replaced black and white. When she opened her eyes again he found himself looking at the old Zoe, the girl he'd known so long ago. No heavy kohl, no mask of makeup—just naturally long lashes and clear green eyes and pale skin.

She reached for a mascara tube and his hand shot out.

"No."

She frowned. "Sorry?"

"You look better without it."

She shook him off and leaned forward to stroke on fresh mascara.

"I think you'd better go. Thanks for looking me up. It was…interesting," she said, her eyes never leaving her own reflection.

He stared at her in the mirror, and she finally looked at him, cocking an eyebrow.

"What? You want more? Okay, thanks for the sex. You rocked my world more than anyone has in a long time. Happy?"

Not by a long shot, but he was beginning to realize that there was no way he was going to get through her defenses tonight. She'd bite her tongue off before she asked for help.

Without another word he turned for the door. He heard her close it behind him as he walked down the corridor. He walked out into rain and an overwhelming sense of guilt.

He'd stood against the bar tonight watching the men around him wanting her, and he'd wanted to hurt every single one of them. Then he'd gone backstage and hammered himself into her as though she really was nothing more than a hot body.

He spat in the gutter but it didn't take away the bad taste in his mouth.

He'd lost control. She'd gone out of her way to provoke him, sure, but it was no excuse. He revved the Mustang hard and left rubber on the road as he pulled into the street. He'd wanted to help her, and instead he'd let his cock do the thinking.

It wasn't going to happen again.

3

ZOE SAT IN HER CHANGE ROOM for a long time after Liam had left.

Slowly she began to gather her things. She didn't bother putting on the rest of her makeup. She simply packed her kit and folded her stage clothes into her gym bag.

She could hear the band talking and laughing in the band room when she entered the corridor. They'd want to keep partying, go grab a burger and some beers in the city like they usually did after a gig. Even though she'd give anything to be able to walk away without talking to another soul, she forced herself to duck in and make her excuses before escaping.

Cool rain misted her cheeks when she stepped out into the night. She raised her face and closed her eyes and let it wash over her. Only when her tank top and jeans were soaked did she cross to her car and throw her gear on the backseat.

It took her ten minutes to drive to her apartment in the inner northern suburb of Essendon. She was shivering by the time she let herself in the front door. She told herself it was because of the rain.

A weak mewl drew her attention to the corner of her small studio apartment and she crouched down to run a hand over the distended belly of the tabby cat she'd found collapsed in her doorway two nights ago.

"How are you doing, little miss? You hungry again? Huh?"

The cat had a collar but no name tag or address, and she'd consumed everything Zoe had put in front of her over the past couple of days. Zoe had no idea when her kittens were due— soon, if the size of the cat's belly was anything to go by. Zoe had made a bed out of an old box and some shredded paper and handwritten some notices and posted them in her neighbors' mailboxes. She hadn't heard anything yet, but surely someone would be looking for their pet? Or had the cat been abandoned when it fell pregnant?

Zoe took the time to open a can of tuna for the cat before shedding her clothes and stepping into the shower. She washed herself carefully, making sure every trace of Liam Masters was removed from her skin. She wanted no reminders of what had happened between them tonight—no traces of his aftershave, nothing.

She hadn't had time for dinner so she opened another can of tuna and ate it straight from the tin. She smiled at the cat as she collected both empty tins and dumped them in the garbage.

"Dinner for two, hey? It's all glamour around here, don't let anyone tell you any different."

The cat simply stared at her with big, unblinking eyes. Zoe crouched beside it again and smoothed her hand over its warm, full body.

"I suppose I should give you a name if you're going to be hanging around for a while. You got any ideas?"

Predictably, the cat didn't have any suggestions.

"How about Lucky?" she said. "Lucky I found you. Lucky you like tuna. What do you think?"

This time the cat turned her head to lick Zoe's hand.

"Well, that's *that* decided, then."

She gave the cat one last pat and stood. She felt restless, edgy. Usually after a gig she was wired for a while, but not like this.

Why had Liam walked back into her life after all these

years? Everything had been good, on an even keel. Then he'd walked in the door and tilted everything off balance.

She crossed to the kitchen to grab the vodka from the freezer. With her back pressed to the cool metal of the fridge door she drank a shot straight up, then another.

Liquid heat burned its way down her throat and into her belly. She closed her eyes, savoring the warmth.

A flash of memory dragged at her: the first hard, thick slide of Liam's body inside hers.

She opened her eyes and poured herself another shot.

She'd meant for the sex to end things, to draw a line under years of hurt and curiosity and wanting. But it hadn't felt like an ending. Not even close.

She climbed into bed and placed the vodka bottle on her bedside table. The fire in her belly was spreading to the rest of her body, making the world fuzzy.

She just wanted to forget. That was all she'd ever wanted. To pretend none of it had ever happened.

Beneath the covers, her fingers found the thin, neat line of the scar on her belly. The line formed the stem of her first tattoo, a work that had evolved into the piece that now traversed her belly and hip and wound its way up her spine to wrap itself around her neck. She traced the scar over and over, then pressed both hands flat over her belly.

Why did you come looking for me, Liam? Why couldn't you just leave me be?

The vodka and the bourbon she'd had earlier joined forces to make her eyelids heavy. She pulled the covers up and switched off the light.

She turned onto her side and hugged her pillow. In the dark, she could hear her clock ticking and the rustle of Lucky moving in her box. Never had she been so grateful for the presence of another living thing.

Tonight was not a night to be alone.

ZOE WAS LATE into work the next morning. Jake didn't say a word but she knew he wasn't happy. Her first client was cooling her heels in the shop, making noises about going somewhere else for the Lady Smurf tattoo she wanted on her butt, for Pete's sake. Zoe turned on the charm and had the client smiling in no time.

Zoe had fallen asleep without turning on her alarm clock last night. She wasn't quite sure how that had happened, although the whole drinking-herself-into-a-stupor thing probably had something to do with it. She didn't usually drink alone. Not for a long time, anyway.

She blamed Liam. Why the hell not, after all? She blamed him for so many other, more important things.

She'd had sex with him last night. She still couldn't quite get her head around it. She'd finally experienced the ultimate intimacy with him, had him inside her body. Twelve years too late to mean anything to anyone. Certainly not to her.

She finished Lady Smurf then started inking in the color on a full-back tattoo for a regular client. By lunchtime she'd regained her equilibrium. Jake was talking to her again and she bought him lunch at the local pizza place by way of a suck-up.

Then Liam walked in the door late in the afternoon and her stomach bottomed out. He was carrying a bunch of flowers—lilies and roses and some purple flower she didn't recognize. Jake smirked when he saw them. Zoe frowned.

"No," she said before he could open his mouth.

"You don't know what I'm here for," Liam said.

"It doesn't matter. I'm not going to sleep with you again, I don't like flowers, and I don't want to talk to you. Unless you were planning on just standing there and breathing, I think you're all out of options."

"I want a tattoo," he said.

She stared at him. There was no way he'd come in here looking for a tattoo, she'd bet a month's pay on it.

"Marking yourself for life is a pretty serious decision, not an impulse purchase," she said.

Liam turned his back and grasped the waistband of his T-shirt, lifting it up to display his back. She tore her gaze from his broad shoulders and impressive lats long enough to note he had three tattoos already—some kind of motorcycle gang insignia high on his left shoulder, three lines of gothic writing in latin on his right, and a dragon low on his tailbone. She stepped closer to check them out.

"Dragon's nice. This insignia's a bit ropey, though. You've got color missing, bleeding lines."

Standing this close, she could smell the fresh sunshiny scent of whatever detergent he washed his clothes in.

She stepped back and he turned to face her.

"Can you fit me in?"

"No," she said, crossing her arms over her chest.

Jake cleared his throat behind her.

"Dock my pay," she said without turning around.

"What's wrong, Zoe? Scared I might talk you into something you don't want to do?" Liam asked.

"How old do you think I am? You really think a dare's going to make me change my mind?"

He slid the tips of his fingers into the front pockets of his jeans and let his weight rock back on his heels, waiting.

"You don't know me," she said, stabbing a finger at him.

"I know that."

"You're not going to talk me into anything."

"Whatever you say."

She glared at him, then swiveled on her boot heel.

"You'd better not be one of those wimpy guys who gets

all sooky at the first bite of the needle," she said as she strode through to the workroom.

"Hallelujah," Jake said.

Liam followed her through and watched while she set up her workstation.

"What do you want and where do you want it?" she asked as she banged the autoclave shut.

He lifted his T-shirt and tapped his lower belly.

"Think you could copy my company logo?" he asked, pulling a business card from his back pocket.

She studied the card, flicking it with her thumbnail. Masters Mechanics in blocky graffiti text. Glossy black card stock. Impressive. He must be doing well.

"I can do this. Pretty sensitive area, though."

"You've got a tat on your belly."

"I'm tougher than you."

He smiled. "Sure you are."

She tore the plastic off a fresh set of ink cups.

"You want it in color?"

"What do you think would look best?"

She considered for a minute. It was tempting to punish him by branding him with an ugly tattoo, but she had her professional pride.

"Blackwork, lots of shading. It'll jump," she said.

"Good. Where do you want me?"

She adjusted the client chair, tilting it back so he'd be reclined in front of her.

"On your back, shirt off. You can take your jeans off or just pull them down. Your choice."

She'd seen hundreds of guys strip for tattoos. She'd tattooed asses, groins, thighs, chests. She'd seen it all.

But she hadn't seen Liam Masters without his shirt on for a very long time. She forced herself not to stare as he pulled his

T-shirt over his head. He had big, defined pec muscles, the kind that came from manual labor, not the gym. His abdominal muscles rippled beneath his skin as he climbed into the chair.

She looked away when he undid the stud on his jeans, fiddling with her gun and needles. When she looked back, he had his jeans unzipped and spread wide, the top of his boxer-briefs rolled down, his lower belly fully exposed. She stared at the crisp dark curls arrowing down his flat, hard belly, then darted a quick glance at the thicker hair growing at the top of his pelvic bone.

"I'm going to have to shave you," she said.

He shrugged. She grabbed the old-fashioned boar's bristle shaving brush she preferred and lathered him up. His skin was firm and resilient beneath her hands as she shaved the left side of his belly from navel to just above his groin.

He lay back with one arm crooked behind his head the whole time, watching her.

"So, how's Tom? What's he up to these days?" he asked as she dried him off.

She gave him a look. "We're not talking about my family."

"Why not?"

"Because I don't want to. Because it's my life and you're not a part of it."

He was silent as she prepared a spirit master transfer of his company logo.

"I don't think you should go any bigger than this," she said when she displayed the finished image.

The design she was proposing was approximately three inches across and would sit snugly between the midline of his belly and his hip bone.

"I trust you," he said.

She snorted. "There's your first mistake. Never trust anyone, Liam. You should know that by now."

She pulled on fresh gloves, poured ink and prepped his belly with alcohol before applying the spirit transfer to his skin. Clear purple lines were left behind when she peeled off the transfer.

She smoothed Vaseline over the top to keep his skin lubricated while she worked. Then she reached for her tattoo gun.

Her hand was shaking. Her hands never shook when she worked. Ever. She could feel Liam watching her. She met his eyes.

"Now's the time to back out," she said.

"I trust you," he said again.

She shook her head and pressed the foot pedal to turn the machine on. Then she placed a hand on his warm, firm belly and held his skin taut while she pressed the needle into his body.

He didn't tense or flinch like some people. He simply lay there, utterly relaxed, watching her. He waited until she had completed the initial outline before speaking again.

"What can we talk about, then?" he asked. "Tell me what's not out of bounds."

She kept her eyes on her work. She was acutely aware of him, more so than she'd ever been with any other client. The warm soapy smell of him, the muscles beneath his skin, the occasional brush of his pubic hair against her forearm as she shifted around.

"The weather. Football. The state of the economy. Pick a topic," she said.

"What about your work? Can we talk about that?"

She shrugged and kept working.

"Are you any good?" he asked.

"Fine time to ask me that," she scoffed. She lifted the needle from his skin as his belly flexed with laughter.

"I already know you're good. You never did anything by halves," he said. "I just wanted to hear you say it."

She used some paper towel to wipe ink away and took a moment to scan the design. It was coming along well.

"You think I have an ego problem?" she asked. "You think I need some positive reinforcement, is that it?"

She glanced up at him and got caught for a moment in his deep brown eyes.

"I don't think your ego is the problem, but something is."

She smiled as she sat back and stretched out her lower back.

"There's Dudley Do-Right. I was wondering when he'd rear his ugly head. Give it up, Liam. I don't need to be fixed."

"You're not happy," he said.

Her hand clenched around the tattoo machine.

"And you are?"

He shrugged. "This isn't about me."

"I see. You can dish it but you can't take it."

"Sorry to interrupt the love-in," Jake said from the doorway. She looked up to see him standing with his jacket in hand. "I've locked up the front. See you tomorrow. On time, okay?"

She rolled her eyes. He waved to Liam, then he was gone.

Leaving them alone.

Instantly the tension that had been humming quietly between them took on new life.

"I'm just going to change needles. You need to use the bathroom or anything?"

"I'm good."

She watched out of the corner of her eye as he shifted his hips. She flushed hot as a memory hit her from last night—the bone-jarring strength of him as he thrust into her, over and over.

She dropped the needle pack she'd just opened and swore.

"Problem?"

"No," she said.

She grabbed another sterile needle pack and loaded up a

five mag to shade his tattoo. She sprayed him down with alcohol again, put on fresh gloves and met his eyes for the first time in five minutes.

"Ready to go again?"

"Whenever you are."

For the next hour she brought Liam's tattoo to life, using various shades of black to shadow and enhance the design. He remained silent throughout, but she was aware of him watching her, studying her face, her hands, her body.

Finally she sat back and wiped his tattoo one last time.

"Done."

"Can I look?"

She passed him a hand mirror and he inspected the tattoo.

"Yeah." He nodded approvingly. "Like you said, the black-work really makes it pop."

Warmth filled her cheeks. Great, now she was flattered that he liked her work. Next she'd be whittling his name in a tree trunk.

"Okay, care and feeding of your new tattoo," she said in a brisk, no-nonsense voice. "I'm going to put some antibiotic cream on it and bandage it, and I want you to keep it covered for tonight, then soak the bandage off tomorrow morning."

She filled him in on the rest of the instructions for taking care of himself and handed over a leaflet that covered everything she'd said.

"Got it?"

"You're very thorough. Think I just got slapped on the ass and sent home last time I had ink done."

She shrugged. Like he'd said, she didn't do things by half measures.

She reached for the antibiotic cream and squeezed some onto her fingertips. He flinched and grabbed her wrist when she applied it to his skin.

"That's cold," he said.

"Poor baby," she said, mostly because she was suddenly very aware that the tattoo was finished and he was still half undressed and she was wholly turned-on.

She'd admitted it to herself last night, hadn't she? Sex with Liam had felt like a beginning, not an ending.

She twisted her wrist in his grasp and he let go, sinking slowly back onto the chair. She smoothed the lotion onto his hot, hard belly, her movements slower than they strictly needed to be. He felt good.

She slid a look his way. He was watching her hand, his jaw doing the same tense thing that it had last night when she'd put her hand down her panties.

When she glanced back at his body, a significant bulge had developed in the crotch of his jeans. She squeezed her thighs together, anticipating what was going to happen next.

She hadn't wanted to see him again. She didn't want to talk to him about old times or new times or anything to do with herself and her life. But she wanted him inside her again so much that a needful ache had started to throb between her thighs.

There were so many things she would never have in her life—a family, a husband, a home full of laughter and love. She figured she deserved whatever brief moments of satisfaction or pleasure she could grab along the way.

She reached for the self-adhesive bandage that she'd cut to size earlier and stuck it to his skin, smoothing the edges with her fingers. Only when he was protected did she allow her hand to slide into the gaping fly of his jeans and onto his erection. She'd barely wrapped her fingers around him before his hand was on her wrist again.

She smiled slightly. "Haven't we played this game before? I can tell you who'll win."

She tried to stroke him but he pulled her hand free of his jeans.

"No," he said.

She couldn't understand why he was being coy. He wanted it, she wanted it. Even she could do the math.

"You've got to be kidding. You come here, you lie there for two hours with my face practically in your crotch, and now you're not going to follow through?"

"I'm not going to sleep with you, Zoe. Last night was a mistake. I didn't come here today looking for sex. I want to be your friend."

She stared at him, then pointed a finger at his still-bulging groin.

"Bullshit."

He shrugged, unabashed. "Yeah, I'm hard for you. You're hot. Last night was hot. But that's not why I'm here. I want you to trust me again. I want you to talk to me."

His words were so confronting, so terrifying that she jerked back in her seat.

"I knew I shouldn't have said yes to the tattoo," she said.

She stood and started gathering up the discarded paper towel and used ink cups. She heard him dressing behind her, and a wave of old, old humiliation swept over her. It was just like before. She'd thrown herself at him and he'd pushed her away.

She closed her eyes as she remembered last night, how she'd had to strip and touch herself before she had provoked him into taking action.

Liam didn't want her.

He'd never really wanted her the way she wanted him.

But she'd always known that, hadn't she? She'd known it the moment she woke up the day after her ill-fated vigil to find that he'd gone in the night without so much as a goodbye and good luck, let alone an explanation.

He didn't want her. And she'd been so heartbroken over him that she'd thrown herself away and ruined her life in the process.

Suddenly all the fear and pain and regret and self-hate rose up inside her. She clenched her hands and closed her eyes and thumped her fists down onto her work surface.

"Get out! Get out of here before I call the goddamn cops," she said.

LIAM STARED at Zoe's tense back. Her head was bowed, her fists pressed into the counter in front of her. She looked like she was ready to either explode or fall apart.

"Zoe," he said, putting a hand on her shoulder.

She shuddered as though she couldn't stand to have him touch her, and he slid his hand free.

"I want you out of here and I never want to see you again, all right?" she said.

She still hadn't turned around. He couldn't see her face and he was almost glad he couldn't.

"Tell me what's going on, Zoe," he said.

"Why should I tell you anything? You gave up the right to be my friend, to talk to me, to know me, when you pissed off in the middle of the night without even saying goodbye."

He hated this. She was quivering with emotion she was wound so tight. He wanted to take her in his arms and soothe her. He wanted to kiss her, calm her. Do whatever it took to take away the raw hurt in her voice and the tense defensiveness in her body.

"You were fifteen years old, Zoe. And I was bad news. I did it for your own good," he said.

She swore.

"I want you out of here," she said again. "Just go."

He stared at her back for a long moment, then finally reached for his coat.

"What do I owe you for the tattoo?" he asked.

She gave a sharp, empty laugh that sounded dangerously

close to tears. He didn't know what else to do or say, so he exited to the front of the parlor and left three hundred dollars on the counter, all the cash he had on him. He unbolted the door and crossed to his car, waiting until he saw Zoe lock the front and turn off the lights before he drove away.

Never in his life had he felt so helpless. Even watching his mother die had been less painful than this. Then he'd known there was nothing he could do. With Zoe his gut told him he could help her, or that he at least had to try, but he had no clue where to start. The only interaction she seemed prepared to tolerate with him was sex, and he refused to go there again with her. He had nothing to offer her, not long-term. He'd only wind up hurting her more than he already had.

He couldn't face the thought of going home. Instead, he went to the workshop and got stuck into his in-tray.

Vinnie had left the forms for the biker build-off comp on his desk and he filled them out and wrote a check to cover the entry fee. He tried to concentrate on the work insurance policies his admin manager had asked him to review, but his mind kept reverting to thoughts of Zoe.

There was no way he could leave things the way they were.

He tossed the insurance paperwork to one side and drew his computer keyboard toward himself. First he tried the white pages, but there were more than fifty listings for T. Ford in Melbourne. He flicked to a new screen. He was no computer guru, but he knew how to do a Google search. He typed in Tom's name, along with Melbourne, Australia. He trawled through three pages before he found a hit that looked interesting—a listing for Tom Ford, accountant, talking at a recent small-business conference. Tom had always been good at math, and his father had been an accountant.

It was easy work to find the Web site for the Melbourne

firm Tom worked for, then a contact number for Tom himself. Liam checked the time. It was after eight. No doubt Tom would have gone home for the evening, but at least if he had voice mail, Liam would know if he was onto the right Tom Ford or not.

To his surprise, someone picked up on the second ring.

"I told you I'd be home by nine. Quit bugging me or I'll never get this done," Tom said, light amusement in his tone.

"Tom, it's Liam Masters calling. I'm not sure if you remember—"

"Damn. Liam. My God. Of course I remember you." Tom sounded stunned but not unhappy to hear from him.

Liam's shoulders dropped as he let go of an unspoken fear: that Tom would still be angry with him after all these years.

"I've thought about you a lot, wondered where you wound up," Tom said.

"Me, too," Liam said.

"Wow. This is a real blast from the past," Tom said. "I don't suppose you want to catch up? I mean, is that why you're calling?"

Liam stood and stared out through the safety-glass window of his office into the workshop.

"I did want to talk to you, actually. About Zoe," he said.

"Right." Liam didn't miss the wariness in the other man's tone.

"I ran into her the other day," Liam said.

Tom gave a hard laugh. "Yeah? Where was that, at the tattoo parlor or one of the thrash clubs?" He sounded resigned and sad.

Liam decided to take a punt. "What are you doing now? Can I come talk to you?" he asked.

Tom hesitated for a beat. "Sure. Let me call home and tell Jane I'll be later than I expected."

"You're married?"

"Yep. Three kids and a dog, too. How about you?"

"None of the above."

Tom gave him his work address and told him the best place to find parking.

"Call me from the street when you get here and I'll buzz you in."

Liam drove into the city and along St. Kilda Road, his gut churning all the way. He was nervous about seeing Tom. There had been a handful of people in Liam's life who stood out as good, decent people, and Tom was one of them. So were his parents and his sister. And Liam had repaid them by falling in love with Zoe and almost taking her innocence, then bailing on them in the middle of the night with little or no explanation.

Tom's firm had offices in a modern metal and glass tower. The foyer was marble, the elevator chrome and plush carpet. Tom was waiting for him when the doors opened on the twentieth floor.

They shook hands, each taking stock of the other. Tom's hair was darker than the sandy brown Liam remembered, and he'd bulked up from the skinny seventeen-year-old he'd once been. There were lines around his eyes and mouth, and his dress sense had improved. He looked good. Happy, healthy, prosperous.

"Man, look at you. You're huge," Tom said, eyeing Liam's shoulders.

"Working with metal will do that," Liam said.

Tom led him to a nicely furnished corner office. Built-ins filled with serious-looking books lined one wall, while the other wall was given over to a series of bright, attention-grabbing paintings, stylized streetscapes of Melbourne in vibrant colors. Tom gestured him toward the couch and took an armchair opposite him.

"Can I get you a drink? There's beer, some wine."

"I'm good, thanks," Liam said.

Tom smoothed his hands down the thighs of his suit pants then took a deep breath.

"I've been thinking about this for a long time, so I'm just going to say it. I'm sorry I hit you that night. I was way out of line, and I want you to know that I regretted it the moment I went inside. Even more when I woke up the next morning and you were gone and I realized you were serious about leaving because of Zoe," Tom said.

Liam shifted in his chair. "You did the right thing," he said.

"No, I didn't. You were family, man. I let you down. It used to kill me, thinking about what happened to you."

There was a question in Tom's eyes. Liam leaned forward so he could ease a business card from his back pocket. He handed it over.

"Stop giving yourself a hard time. I did okay," he said. "Got about thirty people working for me now. Last year's turnover was around ten mill."

Tom stared at the card, an incredulous smile on his face.

"No way. My boss bought one of your custom choppers last year. I should have put the pieces together. Masters Mechanics. No wonder Jane tells me I'm hopeless all the time."

"You look like you're doing pretty well yourself," Liam said.

Tom shrugged. "Just your ordinary everyday wage slave. I keep talking about going out on my own, but I don't know if I want the hassle. Life's pretty good at the moment. I get to spend plenty of time with the kids. It's not so bad."

They both nodded and an awkward silence fell, the unspoken issue of Zoe sitting between them now that they'd addressed their own history.

"How was she?" Tom asked. "You didn't say on the phone where you saw her."

Liam wasn't about to tell him about the painting. There were some things a brother didn't need to know.

"I walked into the tattoo parlor, and there she was," he said. It was a version of the truth, after all. "She wasn't very pleased to see me."

"She took your leaving hard. Really hard."

Liam leaned forward, hands clasped loosely together, elbows on his thighs.

"Tell me what happened," he said.

Tom scrubbed his face with his hands and leaned back in his chair.

"Things kind of fell apart for us all after you left. Zoe had some trouble at school. Mom and Dad got divorced. Everything changed."

Liam stared at the other man. "There's more," he said.

Tom nodded. "But it's Zoe's business, not mine. She…had some bad luck. And it changed everything for her. Made her angry. Mom and Dad were stressed-out over it, they started fighting, blaming each other. When they got divorced, I think Zoe saw it as just one more thing she'd screwed up. She ran away from home when she was seventeen. Same age as you, actually."

Liam wasn't surprised. Zoe felt like someone who had been out on her own, fighting her own battles for a long time.

"You know about Sugar Cane and Vixen?" Liam asked.

"Yeah, I know about it."

"I want to help her," Liam said, laying his cards on the table. "I want to try to make things right."

"Why?"

It was a legitimate question. Only the truth would do.

"Because Zoe is special, and I hurt her."

Tom shook his head. "It was a long time ago."

"Still. I care about her. I want her to be happy."

Tom eyed him for a long moment. "You're not married, you said?" he asked.

Liam could see where his mind was going. He shook his head.

Tom broke eye contact. "I just thought… There was obviously something pretty intense between the two of you once upon a time."

Liam flashed to those wild, out-of-control moments in the change room, then to the almost overwhelming temptation she'd offered him tonight.

"Believe me, I can't give Zoe what she needs," he said.

Tom stood and crossed to a minibar and grabbed two beers. He tossed one to Liam, and they each took a mouthful in silence.

"I don't know what to tell you. We've tried everything. She resents any interference. Won't even talk about the band thing. Hasn't seen Mom or Dad for over a year. I think the only reason Jane and I still see her is because of the kids. She's a great aunty."

Tom gestured to the walls.

"She's bloody talented, and she wastes it in that shitty tattoo parlor. She lives in a tiny studio apartment, won't let me buy her a new car. It drives me nuts if I think about it too much."

Liam stood to study the paintings. He'd noticed them the moment he walked in, and a part of his brain had itched with recognition. Zoe's work. He studied the smooth lines, the colors, the distinctive style.

"She did this with an airbrush, yeah?"

"Yeah. But she can work with oils, watercolors. She even did some etchings a few years ago. You should see them. Like I said, a bloody waste."

Liam nodded, an idea forming. "Okay. Good."

Tom glanced at him. "What's good about it?"

"I've got a friend who owns an art gallery. She'd love to see Zoe's work."

Tom shook his head. "She won't accept your help."

Liam smiled. "She will if I make her an offer she can't refuse."

Tom looked uncertain, but Liam could see he wanted to believe. Liam's smile faded as he remembered Zoe's words to him today, her utter repudiation of him and everything he had to offer.

He hoped he wasn't holding out false hope. As he'd learned over the past few days, Zoe Ford was one tough nut to crack.

But he had to try.

4

Zoe came home to a phone message from her brother.

"Zoe, hey. I just wanted to see how you're doing. Jane and I thought it would be nice to catch up on the weekend. We were thinking a barbecue on Sunday if you were up for it. Anyway, give me a call and we'll work something out. We miss you."

It made her belly burn to hear how uncertain and wary her brother sounded. There was a time when they'd been the best of friends. Now, all they seemed to do was fight because Tom wanted to give her things she didn't want or need or because Tom wanted to try to save her from herself.

The last time she'd seen her brother they'd fought over the band. Or, more specifically, Vixen. Sugar Cane had been generating some buzz on the Internet and someone had posted some amateur footage on YouTube. She could still remember the concern in Tom's voice when he'd asked why she felt the need to flaunt herself so blatantly. He didn't understand, and she didn't try to explain it to him. She'd been too busy being angry at him for judging her.

The reminder that she was now estranged from the one member of her family who she'd managed to maintain some kind of a relationship with was enough to make her reach for the bourbon bottle again.

The phone message felt like a shitty cherry on top of a very shitty day. She had to do something to stop herself from thinking. And yet despite her determination to forget, *if onlys* circled her mind like vultures as she drank. She'd learned a long time ago that regrets didn't change a thing but sometimes it was impossible to silence the Greek chorus in her head.

One thing was very clear in her mind, however. She would not be talking to Liam Masters again. That was one decision she was firm on, an absolute no-brainer. He had already caused enough turmoil in her life. She didn't care what he did or said, she was not going to engage with him. And she certainly wasn't going to allow herself to be attracted to him. Which was another good reason for not seeing him again. He'd been her first love as well as her first lust, the man who'd awakened her to sexual desire and need. The first time he'd kissed her, touched her breasts, slid his hands between her legs was burned into her memory, still fresh after all these years. Added to the fact that he'd grown into a ruggedly sexy man— Well, it was best to steer clear of him. She might not be the sharpest pencil in the box, but she knew when she was in a no-win situation.

She lay in bed, four bourbons gone, once again tracing the neat line of her scar. Over and over, as if she could erase it, wish it gone, remove it from her life.

The biggest *if only* of all.

One high-school party. That was all it had taken to change the course of her life.

She'd cried herself to sleep every night for a month after Liam left, hoping against hope that he'd ride up the driveway on his motorbike or at least call or drop a postcard in the mail. But there'd been nothing. It didn't take long for her grief to turn inward. She'd blamed herself for his leaving, for pushing him away with her demands and her declaration of love.

Two months after he'd driven off into the night, Zoe had climbed out her bedroom window and gate-crashed a party she'd heard her brother talking about. She'd gotten drunk—her first time—and done everything she could to attract the attention of one of the boys at the party. Any boy would do, it hadn't mattered to her. She'd been desperate to prove to herself that she was attractive, that what had happened with Liam didn't mean anything, that other boys would want her even if he hadn't.

Marty Johannsen had wanted her. He'd grabbed her around the waist and pulled her onto his knee when she stumbled past him in the backyard. Before she'd known it, she'd been kissing him, his tongue in her mouth, his hands up her top. Nothing like with Liam, any of it. She hadn't felt anything. But Marty hadn't pushed her away—that was the only thing that counted.

She'd kept drinking until she could barely walk. Marty had offered to see her home. On the way, he'd led her into the local park. She didn't object when he pushed her to the ground. She didn't care. She didn't stop him from pulling down her jeans. She simply lay there and bit her lip and tried not to cry out as he pushed himself inside her.

It had hurt, but not much. Afterward he'd waited for her to dress then walked her to the end of her street. She'd told herself she'd exorcised Liam forever as she climbed back in her bedroom window.

Ten weeks later she'd been walking home from school when a crippling pain in her belly had sent her to her knees. She'd felt the warmth of blood between her legs and lost consciousness. When she woke she was attached to tubes and machines in hospital, and her parents were by her bed.

She'd suffered an ectopic pregnancy from her one night of unprotected sex. The fetus had ruptured her right fallopian tube and so badly damaged her uterus that there had been no option but for the surgeon to give her a hysterectomy. At fifteen years and seven months, she had been made sterile.

It had shaped her life. There was no point pretending any different. It had driven her parents apart as they dealt with the aftermath of her pregnancy. It had made her an object of curiosity and fascination at school. And, as she grew into adulthood, her inability to have children had been a stumbling block for every man she met who she could have loved. No one wanted an empty shell.

Zoe reached for the bourbon bottle and poured herself another drink. She told herself it didn't matter. It was what she always told herself and it wasn't strictly true, but it had gotten her through the past twelve years and it would see her through another twelve. She had the band and her art. She had sex whenever she wanted it. She was her own person, in charge of her own destiny. It was enough.

It would have to be.

Dulled by bourbon, she finally drifted to sleep at around midnight.

She was woken at three by Lucky panting and mewling in distress. Zoe scrambled from bed to find the cat sprawled half in, half out of the cardboard box, her eyes full of pain. Zoe knew nothing about cats and kittens, but her gut told her that something was not going according to plan.

She grabbed the phone book and flicked urgently through the listings for veterinary clinics until she found one that offered twenty-four-hour emergency care. She tore the page out, then called a cab. After half a bottle of bourbon, she was in no state to drive. She dragged on the nearest clothes and squatted by Lucky, trying to work out how to move her without causing more pain.

Gently she tried lifting the cat back into the box, but Lucky hissed and struck out at her. Zoe bit her lip and persisted, finally easing the cat onto its side on the shredded paper. The low sound of a car outside told her the taxi had arrived. She grabbed her purse and keys and lifted Lucky's box into her arms.

The cat had gone disturbingly quiet by the time they pulled up outside the clinic. Zoe threw money at the cab driver and ran into the clinic, the box pressed to her belly.

"I need help for my cat," she said. "I think she's in trouble."

A bleary-eyed nurse looked up at her, her expression becoming more alert when she saw the distressed cat.

"Come right through," she said, ushering Zoe toward a door.

Two hours later, Zoe sat staring into space in the waiting room. The vet—Dr. Kent—had been very concerned when he examined Lucky. She was in labor, but her kittens weren't coming. He had warned Zoe that it was possible that neither Lucky nor the kittens would survive the night.

Zoe told herself over and over that it was just a cat. Not even her cat—some stupid stray that someone else hadn't loved enough to look after.

It didn't stop her from wanting to cry, or from wanting to make deals with God or whoever oversaw these kinds of small, everyday tragedies.

Lucky had to be okay. Her kittens had to survive, and Lucky had to live to help them grow up into big, dumb, ugly cats like herself.

It was eight o'clock before Dr. Kent came out to talk to her again. Lucky was the proud mother of four kittens, all of whom were small and undernourished, not unlike Lucky herself. Two boys and two girls. At the moment the kittens were as healthy as could be expected and Lucky was holding her own, but nothing was certain. He advised Zoe to go home, get some rest and call again around lunchtime.

Zoe caught a cab home and crashed almost instantly. When she woke, it was nearly midday. Her first thought was for

Lucky, the second for Jake. Late two days in a row. It wasn't going to be pretty.

She was right. He'd had to cancel two appointments for her, one a lucrative full-chest tattoo that would have netted the parlor good money by the time Zoe had outlined and colored it over several sessions. She explained about the cat, but he didn't care.

"A freaking stray? Are you kidding me? You just cost me two grand today," he said, his face red. "Don't start pissing me around again, Zoe. I won't put up with it."

Zoe stared at him, resenting his reference to the bad old days when she'd first started with him when she'd been drinking heavily and was often late and unreliable.

"I'm not pissing with you. My cat is sick. I'm worried about her."

Jake gave her a searching look. "What is going on with you? You're the last person I'd ever imagine taking in a stray, let alone getting clucky over it."

She stilled. "What's that supposed to mean? That I'm some kind of defective or something?"

"No. Don't be so defensive. I only meant you're hardly the maternal type, are you? No one's ever going to catch you wiping baby snot and changing diapers."

Zoe sucked in a hurt breath. She felt as though he'd hit her, just walked up and punched her in the stomach. She stared at him, a torrent of rage and grief churning inside her. Without a word she started gathering her kit together—her tattoo gun, her design book, her shaving gear—her movements jerky.

"What are you doing?"

"What does it look like?"

"You're quitting? Why?"

"Maybe that's just the kind of woman I am," she said, striding for the door, her arms full.

Jake followed her out to the parking lot.

"Zoe. Whatever I said, I'm sorry."

He kept talking the whole time she packed her car. She ignored him, nearly stalling when she reversed too quickly out of her parking spot.

You're hardly the maternal type, are you?

She couldn't get his words out of her head. She drove straight to the vet clinic, only to be told that Lucky's condition had deteriorated. It was all she could do not to scream and punch something.

She went home because there was nowhere else to go. She paced up and down the small space between her bed and the kitchenette, arms wrapped around her torso. If Lucky died...

She was aware that it wouldn't take Dr. Freud to work out why she felt so connected to a pregnant cat she'd only known for a handful of days, but she honestly didn't know what she was going to do. The thought of losing Lucky felt like one shitty blow too many.

She deserved a break, didn't she? Just one decent roll of the dice in her lifetime.

A knock sounded on her front door. It was probably Jake. She owed him an apology. He'd had no way of knowing that his words would hit home harder than he'd ever intended. She'd never told him about what had happened when she was fifteen.

She pulled her hair back off her forehead, bunching it tightly in one hand as she stared at the door. She really didn't want to talk to anyone right now.

Another knock sounded and she reluctantly moved to open the door.

It wasn't Jake, it was Liam. Filling the doorway with his broad shoulders.

She tried to shut him out but he blocked the door with his

foot. She threw her hands in the air and crossed to sit on the end of the bed. She'd let him say his piece. What could it hurt?

He closed the door and leaned against it. Out of the corner of her eyes she could see him taking stock of her apartment, no doubt noting the pile of dirty clothes in the corner, the bourbon bottle on her bedside table next to the stack of books.

"Jake tells me you quit this afternoon."

"That's right."

"Can I ask why?"

"No."

"He said your cat was sick, too."

Zoe shrugged, not looking at him. "Probably going to die."

Heat burned at the back of her eyes. For a heartbeat she wondered how it would feel to lay her head on Liam's shoulder and simply let go, releasing some of the hurt inside her. His arms would be so strong and sure....

She blinked and sniffed the tears back, clenching her hands against her thighs.

"I'm sorry to hear that," he said.

The bed sagged as he sat beside her.

"Is there anything I can do?" he asked.

"You got a degree in vet science?"

"No."

"Then there's nothing you can do."

He reached for her hand and she let him take it, even though she kept her fingers stiff and unresponsive when he curled his hand around hers.

"I came here to offer you a job," he said.

She turned her head to look at him. A mistake. He was sitting so close she could see the amber flecks in his brown eyes.

How she'd loved him, once. With all her foolish teenage heart.

"Before you tell me to stick my offer where the sun doesn't

shine, hear me out," he said. "We've got a big biker build-off comp coming up. Me and my team have got four weeks to design, build and detail a chopper that will blow the competition out of the water."

She tugged her hand free. "So? What's that got to do with me?"

"I saw Tom last night. I saw the paintings you did in his office."

She was on her feet in no seconds flat.

"You are unbelievable. Which part of 'stay the hell out of my life' don't you understand?"

"I want you to paint our chopper," he said, ignoring her outburst.

He stood and collected something he'd left leaning against the wall near the door—a large black artist's folio. He opened it on her bed, spreading out a series of sketches and computer-generated design specs.

"It's a big competition, lots of makers who want to win. But I really like the style of your work. I think you could give us an edge, bring something different to the table," he said.

Zoe hung back, arms crossed over her chest, refusing to so much as glance at the drawings.

"Let me guess. I'm supposed to be drawn in by the challenge and so intrigued by the drawings I'll say yes."

"Something like that," he agreed easily. "It's a great opportunity. I'm a good boss. The money is nice. I think you'd like working with my team."

He sounded so…reasonable, it infuriated her.

"I don't take charity."

"It's not charity. If I just wanted to give you money, I'd find some other way to do it."

Despite herself she glanced at the drawings, taking in the sweeping curves and angles of the design.

"What makes you think I'd have a clue where to start? I'm a tattoo artist, not a spray painter."

"You're an artist, and you know how to use an airbrush. Most important of all, you're talented," he said.

"No."

"No, you're not talented? Or, no, you're not interested?"

"No, it's not going to work," she said.

He made an impatient gesture with his hand. "You've got something better to do, have you? Some other big plan now that you've quit your job?"

She stared at him.

"Didn't think so," he said.

"Don't you dare judge my life."

He made a rude noise and started gathering up his drawings. "This isn't a life, Zoe, this is an existence. A bloody miserable one, from what I can see. But don't let me stop you from wallowing in your misery. God forbid that anyone try to be a friend and offer you a helping hand."

"Maybe I don't want to be just a friend." The words were out of her mouth before she could stop them. Searing heat rushed into her face. Would she never learn her lesson with this man?

She turned away as Liam took a step toward her. His fingers caught her chin and he forced her to meet his eyes.

"Zoe, I am not what you need right now, trust me. But I am someone who can get your art noticed. Take the job. Win the comp for us. Say yes."

They stood looking into each other's eyes for long, long seconds. She thought about how much he'd rocked her world off its axis in the past few days. She remembered what it had felt like to have his hands and mouth on her. And she relived the moment yesterday when he'd rejected her for the second humiliating time.

Finally she nodded.

"Yes. Okay, I'll do it."

He smiled, a big broad grin that almost knocked her back on her heels it was so dazzling.

"Good. Great."

He tossed the folio back onto the bed.

"Take a look at those. The workshop address is on the first page. I'll expect you at eight tomorrow morning."

"Eight?" Normally she didn't start at the parlor until ten, sometimes eleven.

"You heard me. And bring some of your art with you. Your design book, anything else you've got. We need to have a war council."

He pressed a warm hand to her shoulder, then he was gone. She stared at the drawings on her bed and let out a deep sigh. No matter what she promised herself, Liam kept getting beneath her defenses. And now she'd just agreed to work for him.

She was an idiot. But that was nothing new. She'd always been a fool for Liam Masters, hadn't she?

LIAM FELT SEVENTEEN all over again when Zoe walked into Masters Mechanics the next morning. She was wearing worn jeans, a black T-shirt and scuffed cowboy boots, and every man in the workshop stopped in his tracks to stare at her. Including Liam.

As he watched her breasts bounce and her hips sway, he acknowledged that it was going to be hard to work with her every day and keep his hands to himself. There had been precious few times in his adult life when he'd wanted a woman and couldn't have her, and there'd never been any woman who compelled him as much as Zoe. But she was out-of-bounds. She deserved better. Always had, always would.

She was carrying a two-ring binder and an artist's folio and she stopped and looked around uncertainly until she spotted him in his office doorway.

"You made it," he said.

"Yep."

Her gaze took in the racks of bike parts, the half-assembled frames, the three completed choppers ready for road testing.

"This is a little different from what I was expecting," she said.

"You want a tour? I'll introduce you to the guys at the same time."

"Sure. Where can I dump my stuff?"

He showed her into his office and she left her binder and folio on his desk. She glanced around at the plain white walls and functional furniture, then studied the piles of paperwork on his desk.

"You don't spend a lot of time in here," she said.

It was a statement, not a question.

"As little as possible. I like to keep my hand in on the shop floor."

"You mean you hate admin stuff and making big boys toys is a lot more fun."

"Like I said."

He led her out to the front office and introduced her to the receptionist, accountant and office assistant. His marketing manager, Mathew, hastily ended a phone call and casually drifted out to join them and ensure he scored an introduction. He looked at Zoe like she was edible the whole time they exchanged greetings. Liam gave the other man a dark look and led Zoe into the workshop.

He had four fabricating teams at present, each working on their own projects in separate areas of the large warehouse space. To a man they all transformed from articulate, intelligent human beings into monosyllabic beef heads the moment they were standing in front of Zoe. Liam had never seen a better mass impersonation of drooling apes in all his life. Even Vinnie turned into a goggle-eyed idiot as soon as he was within sniffing distance, and he'd sworn off women for life after his ex-wife divorced him and took the kids.

It wasn't just the way her jeans clung her to her high, firm ass or the length of her legs or the smooth, full thrust of her breasts beneath her T-shirt. Although all those things probably had a lot to do with it. Zoe was sexy. She oozed a sort of unconscious body awareness that had a man imagining her naked almost before he'd registered the clear, direct green of her gaze or the knowing, sarcastic tilt to her mouth.

Liam stood with his arms crossed over his chest and watched as Zoe listened to Vinnie explaining the customer's brief for the half-assembled bike in front of them.

She was a handful, full of attitude, hot as hell. And, as he could attest, an incredibly wild ride. Not that any of his employees would ever get close enough to find that out. Not if they wanted to keep eating with their own teeth.

"They seem like nice guys," she said as he led her to his office.

He grunted.

She gave him a sideways look. He realized she looked tired and belatedly remembered her sick cat.

"How's your cat holding up?" he asked as he took a seat behind his desk and she sat opposite him.

"The vet said she had a good night. If she keeps improving, I can pick her and the kittens up tomorrow night."

"Kittens?"

"Two boys, two girls. I guess I'll have to start looking around for homes for them."

She paused significantly. He kept his face impassive. Cats were not his thing—he was a dog man from way back.

"I'm sure you won't have any problems. You should let the

guys know. Half of them are married with kids. They'd probably jump at the chance to score a free pet."

And no doubt the other half would be prepared to take on an eating, sleeping fur ball if they thought it would score them any points with her.

"Good idea," she said.

He drew the two-ring binder toward him.

"Can I?" he asked.

"Sure."

She sat on the edge of her chair, eyes wary, as he flicked through what was essentially a photographic catalog of her tattoo work. Some of the pieces were truly spectacular, real works of art that made him regret the lack of uniformity of his own ink work.

"Some nice stuff in here," he said. "No wonder Jake was so cut up when I spoke to him yesterday."

She shifted in her seat.

"I owe him an apology. I was pretty nuts yesterday. Wound up about Lucky, tired." She shrugged.

He opened the folio and sat a little straighter when he saw the airbrush artwork inside. Zoe twisted her hands together, a frown on her face as she watched him work his way through the folder.

"I've never had any formal training, so technically they're not great," she said after a few minutes broken only by the sound of him leafing through her art. "In fact, they're pretty amateurish, so if you're freaking out right now worrying about how to let me down gently, just say it. I totally understand."

He looked up at her, noting her tense, ready-to-spring-to-her-feet posture.

"Zoe. These are amazing. If we can come up with a way to adapt your style into three dimensions, we're going to kick ass," he said.

An uncertain, surprised smile flickered across her lips for a second before she got control of it.

"Really?"

"Yeah, really. How can you not know how good these are?"

She sat back in her chair and crossed her legs.

"Well, of course I know they're great, but I couldn't expect a Philistine like you to appreciate them," she said.

God forbid that anyone ever see that Zoe was vulnerable or uncertain or needy.

"You're full of shit, you know that?" he said.

She shrugged a shoulder, but a slow smile stole across her face. He found himself smiling back at her.

"I want to show this stuff to Vinnie and a couple of the other guys, do a round table to see what we can come up with."

"You're the boss."

The nervousness was back in her eyes, but he knew that seeing the guys' reactions to her work was the best medicine for her self-doubt. They weren't the kind of men to blow smoke up someone's backside for no reason. Even if that backside was pretty much the hottest thing around.

He had Vinnie pull together Paul, the lead spray painter, and Kinko, the geeky genius who helped them model their projects virtually on the computer before they ever put hammer to metal.

The five of them sat at the round table in the staff room and passed around Zoe's folio and the design drawings for the competition chopper.

"Hey. You're good," Vinnie said as he studied Zoe's work. "Really good."

Liam gave the other man a hard look.

"Why do you think she's here?" he asked.

Vinnie shrugged a shoulder. Liam knew exactly what he was thinking. He turned to Zoe, who was sitting back taking it all in.

"How do you feel about working up some ideas for us?" he asked.

"Sure. It would help if I had some kind of starting point. Like what your inspiration was when you designed the bike, that sort of thing," she said.

Vinnie leaned forward and launched into a description of the vintage choppers he'd loved as a teenager, explaining how he'd adapted classic elements in the original designs to create a more modern look.

"Liam came up with the idea of using the old Eagle frame we've had kicking around for a while, stretching it out a little. Then we worked together on the design for these formed fenders. You've got a lot of surface area to work with—the fenders, the fuel tank, the oil tank," he said.

"So vintage meets today," Zoe said, jotting ideas down on a notepad. "Old school meets new school."

She pushed her pencil between her lips when she finished writing, sucking lightly on the end. Liam shifted in his seat. He could remember her sucking on his tongue just like that, her fingers digging into his hips and ass as she urged him to pump harder, faster. He could remember the wet slide of his body inside hers, the low moan she'd made as she came....

Aware that his jeans suddenly felt a size too small, Liam tore his gaze away and shifted in his seat again.

"We still got that wrecked Harley out the back?" he asked Paul.

"Yeah. Davo started stripping it for parts the other day, but we haven't got around to finishing it yet."

"Let's give the gas tank to Zoe for a practice run." Liam turned to her. "That way you can experiment a little, get used to the curves and angles, try out a few ideas."

She was nodding. "Thanks. I'd really appreciate that."

The meeting broke up and Zoe followed Paul out to collect the Harley tank. Liam watched them walk away, talking and laughing easily.

Zoe was comfortable around men. She always had been—she'd been a tomboy growing up, and he bet she still didn't own a single skirt. Not that she was unfeminine in any way. She was one of those rare women who could hang out with the guys without ever being in danger of becoming one of them.

"Man, she's gorgeous, eh?" Vinnie said beside him.

Liam eyed his chief designer. "Don't even think about it."

Vinnie held up both hands.

"Hey, I'm not a complete moron. I know better than to horn in on the boss's woman."

Liam frowned and turned to face him full-on.

"She's not my woman. She's an old friend. A family friend."

"Sure she is."

Liam swore. "Is it too much to ask for you to keep your mind out of the gutter for five seconds? How about a little respect?"

Vinnie smirked and shook his head. "Oh, man."

"What?"

"Nothing."

Vinnie was still smirking when he moved off to rejoin his team.

Liam slammed the door to his office and did a lap before he admitted to himself that he wanted to follow Paul and Zoe out into the yard and shadow their every step, just in case Paul tried any moves on her.

Which was ridiculous, not to mention embarrassing.

He ran a hand through his hair and glanced around his office for distraction. His gaze fell on the wall clock. It was barely ten. He had a whole day left of watching Zoe interact with his almost all-male staff, then another three weeks and four days after that.

Shit.

He watched through the glass wall of his office as Paul and Zoe returned, Paul carrying the tank for her. Paul said something and Zoe laughed loudly, then punched him on the arm. The look Paul gave her was so full of speculative lust that Liam couldn't help himself. He left his office and strode to meet them.

"Thanks for that, Paul. I'll show Zoe where she can set up," he said coolly.

Paul looked startled at the abrupt dismissal.

"Um, sure. Okay," he said, heading back to the spray booth.

"He's a funny guy," she said.

"Yeah. Hilarious."

He found her an unused workbench and helped her set up her airbrush with one of their air compressors.

"Paul said he'd help me out with any paints or whatever I might need," she said.

I bet he did.

"Great. I'll leave you to it, then," he said.

Zoe was already opening her sketch pad to a fresh page. She glanced up at him when he remained standing at her side.

"Was there something else?" she asked.

His gaze traveled over her face, taking in her smooth skin, the fullness of her bottom lip, the small, puzzled frown between her eyebrows.

"No."

Calling himself ten different kinds of fool, he strode back to his office. Had he really signed on for four weeks of this?

Shit.

ZOE WAS NERVOUS. No point denying it, even if only to herself. Her hands were trembling as she assembled her air gun. She wanted to live up to the trust Liam had put in her. She wanted to be as good as he seemed to think she was.

Who was she kidding? She wanted to impress him, knock him on his ass with her talent and skill.

Which was exactly why it had been so foolhardy to take on this job. She had too much history with Liam for things to ever be cut-and-dried between them.

For the twentieth time that day, her gaze swept the huge warehouse that was home to Masters Mechanics. She'd been impressed by his shiny, professional business card, but this was something else altogether. She'd counted over twenty-five staff this morning and was sure there were more she hadn't met yet.

When Liam had told her he built bikes, she'd imagined a small workshop and a couple of guys—including Liam—in overalls and grease. Not this place, with its gleaming concrete floors and racks of shiny bike parts and busy, productive build crews.

Liam was a success. A big success. No wonder he was in a position to offer to help her out. And no wonder she was feeling so intimidated and nervous that she was stalling, fooling around with her equipment rather than getting into real work.

She pushed her air gun to one side impatiently and pulled her sketch pad toward herself. At the top of the page she wrote "old school" and "tradition" in big bold letters. She tapped her pencil against her teeth for a few seconds, then added the word "today."

An idea formed and she sketched out a rough shape. She cocked her head, considering. Then she shook her head and flipped to a new page. She drew her stool closer to the work bench and bent over the book, drawing in earnest.

Three hours later she was startled when someone nudged her with an elbow.

"Hey, Zoe. You going to stop for lunch or what?" Paul

asked. He peered over her shoulder at her work, his eyebrows rising toward his hairline. "Hey. Awesome."

"It's just ideas," she said.

"Rockin' ideas," he said. "Come on, a group of the guys are walking up to the local burger joint."

Zoe shot a glance toward Liam's office, then immediately gave herself a mental kick. He was too busy to have lunch with her. Plus she was his employee now. She was stupid to even think of it.

"Sure."

She grabbed her wallet and joined the small group of men waiting for her on the sidewalk. There was still some warmth in the sun even though it was May, and she was warm by the time they reached the restaurant. The guys went out of their way to make her feel welcome, doing their best to make her laugh and advising her on which burger was the best. She wasn't stupid—she knew that there was a certain amount of sexual interest in their attention. But she'd always had the knack of making friends with men. She didn't flirt and she wasn't a cock-tease. Pretty soon most guys got the message that she wasn't an easy lay.

When they returned to the workshop Liam was standing in front of his office talking on his cell phone. His gaze scanned her from head to toe before taking in the half-dozen men walking with her. He didn't say a word, just walked into his office and shut the door. She stared at the closed door, wondering what it was that she'd seen in his eyes before he put the door between them.

Jealousy?

No. She'd made it clear he could have her again any number of times and he'd turned her down. She must have been mistaken.

She spent the afternoon refining her ideas on the sketch pad but was constantly distracted by her stupid awareness of everything that Liam said and did—who he was talking to, where he was standing, what he was saying. She didn't want to be, but she was.

She'd seen a new side to him today. The Liam she'd known twelve years ago had been a quiet, intense loner, a young man grieving for his mother and trying to pull his life together. He'd survived a brutal childhood dodging his abusive father's blows, and he'd been touchingly grateful for the small, every-day kindnesses the Fords had shown him. She'd fallen in love with the moments of vulnerability she'd seen in him, with his innate strength and goodness, and, yes, with his handsome good looks and lean, muscular body.

The adult Liam still had the air of a loner. He was still intense. But there was a confidence in him now, a quiet certainty to everything he did. He knew who he was, understood his place in the world. Probably because he'd carved it out himself.

He was an admirable man. Sexy, strong, determined. The kind of man a woman could build a life with.

She smiled bitterly to herself as she stared down at her sketch pad. Build a life. Who was she kidding? She had nothing to offer a man like Liam, or any man, for that matter.

She closed her eyes for a long moment.

Can't change the past, Zoe, she told herself. She knew it was true, but sometimes…

It had been a long time since she'd cried for herself, but the advent of Liam in her life had awakened all the old hurts. She made her way to the bathroom and sat on the closed toilet lid, her hands gripping her knees as she blinked back tears.

After a while she took a deep belly breath and let it out slowly. Life went on, the world kept turning. She'd learned that lesson long ago.

She left the bathroom and went back to her workbench.

She had work to do. Liam was relying on her. She might have screwed up a lot of things in her life, but she was determined not to let him down.

5

LIAM WATCHED ZOE all day. While he was on the phone he watched her. While he was supposed to be helping Vinnie work out a design problem on a high-end custom job, he watched her. If he wasn't looking at her, he was listening to her talking to his staff, charming them with her up-front honesty and down-to-earth sense of humor. Every time the low husk of her laughter sounded in the workshop his gut tightened.

It was driving him crazy. She was driving him crazy. Something had to give.

At six that evening, Vinnie and a few of the guys road-tested a bike. They always took completed commissions for a spin before handing them over to the customer, testing brakes, steering, suspension, comfort of ride. It was a good time for the team—they liked to see the results of their hard work speeding down the road.

He was on the phone when he saw Vinnie call Zoe out to join the gang. He moved to the doorway of his office to keep her in sight, unable to help himself, even as he assured a customer that his bike would be ready on time.

Zoe was laughing as Vinnie encouraged her to get on the bike. Liam couldn't hear what she was saying, but he could read her body language. She couldn't ride, she was scared she'd do something wrong. The men formed a circle around the bike, each offering his own advice on what she should do.

After a few minutes she slid one long leg over the bike's saddle and reached for the handle bars. The guys let up a cheer when she revved the engine. Then Vinnie swung a leg over in front of her and encouraged Zoe to slide her arms around his waist. Someone passed her a helmet, then she and Vinnie shot out into the street in a streak of shiny chrome.

Liam ended the phone call and walked to the front of the workshop to await their return. His jaw was clenched so tightly his teeth ached. He kept seeing Zoe sliding her arms around Vinnie's waist. It was a repeat of lunchtime when she'd been surrounded by a group of hopeful, horny men— it made him feel just a little bit crazy.

He fisted his hands beneath his armpits and kept them there when the bike turned back into the driveway ten minutes later. The guys gathered around to discuss the ride with Vinnie as Zoe slid off the bike. She pulled off the helmet and shook out her hair, laughing all the while.

She was desire personified, sex on legs, sin in human form. She was too much.

"Zoe," he said. "Can I have a word?"

He jerked his head to indicate she should follow him and headed for his office. He waited until she was standing in front of his desk before speaking.

"This is a place of business, in case you hadn't noticed."

She stared at him. "I'm aware of that. Is there some kind of problem?"

"Not yet, but there will be if you keep sashaying around shaking your ass for all the guys. This isn't your stage show. You're not here to impress anyone except me."

Her hands found her hips. "Excuse me?"

"You heard me. I want you in work clothes tomorrow. No more tight jeans. No more tiny little T-shirts. I don't care what you do in your spare time, but on my dime the guys don't need to be distracted."

She glared at him. Her jaw worked for a moment, then her chin came up. "You finished?"

"Yeah, I think so."

He'd been expecting more from her, some lip, more fight. But she didn't say another word, simply turned on her heel and left his office.

He rubbed the bridge of his nose, exhaling deeply. Maybe now he could get a little peace, a little sanity back into his life. Maybe if he didn't have her gorgeous body shoved in his face all day, he'd be able to keep a grip on his need for her.

He should have known better. He should have known Zoe better, at the very least.

The next morning she strutted into work wearing a leather miniskirt, stilettos and the tiny leather vest he'd last seen onstage at Thrashed. Her eyes were smoky with kohl, her lips a deep, throbbing red. She'd straightened her hair so that it hung iron-straight around her face and down her back. The look she gave him was pure defiance as she walked to her workstation, hips swaying provocatively.

It was early and half the guys weren't in yet. The few who were took one disbelieving, appreciative look before hastily turning away. Smart men.

Liam felt his blood begin to boil as she bent over her workbench, her long legs on display. He could almost see the lower curves of her ass, her skirt was so short. He didn't know what he wanted to do more—spank her or get her naked as quickly as humanly possible.

"Zoe," he said from his office doorway. "In here, now."

She threw him a look over her shoulder. "In a minute. I need to sort some stuff out."

She sauntered casually toward the paint storeroom, her

high heels clicking on the floor. He swore under his breath, his temper getting the better of him as he strode after her.

He caught up with her easily and grabbed her by the upper arm, hauling her into the filing room, the nearest available space with a door. She shook his hand free as he kicked the door shut. He didn't want any witnesses when he gave her a piece of his mind.

"What the hell do you think you're doing?" he asked.

"Proving a point."

"I warned you. I told you I didn't want my men distracted."

"Your men. Are you sure that's who we're talking about, Liam? Because I'm willing to bet that exactly the same amount of work got done yesterday, to exactly the same standard as usual, despite me being around. I'm willing to bet that the only man with a problem with me is you."

He glared at her. "You look like a hooker."

"Today I do. Yesterday I didn't. Interesting that you can tell the difference."

She held his gaze, daring him to deny it.

"Your T-shirt was too tight," he said.

Even he could hear how lame he sounded.

"No, it wasn't. Your T-shirt is tighter. I can see every ripple on your chest through the bloody thing."

He glanced down at himself, frowning. "Your jeans were a size too small. All the guys were staring at your ass."

"They'd have been staring at my ass no matter what I was wearing, no matter how I looked. I'm the only female on the workshop floor, for Pete's sake."

"That's bullshit. No man can look at you without wanting to get you naked and you know it."

She frowned, tilting her head to one side as she studied him. After a long moment a slow, cynical smile curled her lips.

"I get it. You don't want me, but no one else can have me."

He swore and ran a hand through his hair. Why did dealing with Zoe always make him feel so out of control?

"This has got nothing to do with what I want or don't want."

"Okay, fine. Then I'll just go out and get to work, then," she said.

She took a step forward and paused, clearly waiting for him to get out of the way.

"You're not working dressed like that."

"I thought we agreed that it wasn't about what you wanted or didn't want?"

She tried to push past him and he grabbed her by the shoulders.

"Jesus, Zoe. What do you want from me? What do you want to hear? Of course I want to sleep with you again. I'm not a freaking saint. But I've already told you that it's a bad idea."

She stared at him. Despite all the makeup and her hard-as-nails clothes and attitude, he could see the vulnerability and uncertainty in her.

"Why? Why is it a bad idea, Liam?"

There was a raw note to her voice, a neediness that undid him.

"Because once I start I might not be able to stop," he said.

"Maybe I don't want you to stop. Ever thought about that?"

His gaze dropped to her mouth. "Every goddamn minute of every goddamn day."

Then he pulled her into his arms and kissed her.

ZOE CLOSED HER EYES as Liam's tongue slid along hers. He tasted of coffee and desire and her whole body went up in flames.

His arms slid around her, his palms firm on her back as he held her close and kissed her. She fisted her hands in his

T-shirt and hung on as he angled her head, seeking more from her. She could feel his hard-on against her belly and she pressed her hips forward, rubbing herself against him.

His hips pressed back, grinding into her. He left her mouth, kissing his way across her cheekbone to her neck. He pulled an earlobe into his mouth, sucking and biting on it gently. Her belly clenched.

"Please, Liam," she whispered as he traced the neckline of her vest with a finger. He unbuttoned her top and spread it wide, pressing his face into her cleavage. She felt his breath on her skin, a warm, steamy rush of air.

"So hot," he murmured as he nuzzled her breast through the silk of her black bra. She shuddered as he opened his mouth over her nipple, pulling it, silk and all, into his mouth.

Her knees were weak she was so turned-on. She clutched at him for support.

"Easy, baby," he said against her skin. His hands slid down to cup her backside, holding her against him.

She could feel the firmness of his thighs against hers, the rasp of his stubble on her skin, the tension in his fingers as he gripped her ass.

She wanted more. A lot more.

She slid her hands down his back to find his butt, cupping a cheek in each hand. He was so round, so firm. She gripped him through his jeans, circling her hips.

Liam made a frustrated noise and used his teeth to tug her damp bra cup down. The heat of his mouth on her bare nipple made her gasp.

"I need to be inside you, Zoe," Liam said against her breast.

It was a question as well as a statement of desire.

"That's what I want, too," she said.

He walked her backward to where a table rested against the rear wall, lifting her and placing her on it. She opened her legs for him, welcoming him between them. He tugged her bra off her shoulders then reached behind her to unclip it. His gaze was hot and hungry as he looked from one breast to the other. She'd never felt more desirable or sexy in her life.

His hands found her knees and she shivered as his thumbs made small, gentle circles on the sensitive skin of her inner legs, his gaze still fixed on her breasts.

"I can't decide what I want to do first," he said, his voice so low it was barely audible.

"Let me give you a hint," she said. She took his right hand and slid it up her thigh until she was pressing it against the damp satin of her panties.

His fingers curled into her, finding the edge of her underwear. She bit her lip as he slipped a finger beneath the elastic.

He groaned and lowered his head to kiss her as his single finger explored between her thighs. She started to pant, already close to losing it.

"Zoe, I'm sorry, I have to see you properly," Liam said. "I've been thinking about you so much…"

"Whatever you want."

She loved how out of control he sounded, how desperate. She wanted him to want her, to need her as much as she needed him.

She watched with hooded eyes as he dropped to his knees in front of her. He pushed up her skirt, reaching for the sides of her panties. She lifted her butt and he slid them down her hips and over her legs. Then he was spreading her legs wide again, his expression caught somewhere between pleasure and pain as he looked at her.

His eyes lifted to meet hers for one brief, intense moment before he leaned forward. She braced her weight back on her arms as she watched his dark head draw closer and closer.

The first touch of his tongue nearly sent her over the edge.

Her whole body jerked and Liam's hands clamped on her thighs. He pressed closer, his tongue hot and wet and fast against her as he kissed her with big, greedy openmouthed hunger.

Too quickly she felt her climax rising inside her. She fought it, wanting to savor every last second. Liam's hands slid up the outside of her thighs to her hips to draw her closer again. She tried hard to hold out, but he was so avid, so intense…

Her back arched and her thighs trembled as she came, her hips pushing against the grip of his hands. He rode out her orgasm and kept kissing her, still hungry for more.

She gasped, quivering with arousal. It was too much. He was too much. She grabbed a handful of his hair and used it to drag his head up. His gaze was unfocused, his expression distracted as he looked up at her.

"Liam. Are you trying to kill me?" she panted.

He looked dazed for a second, then he smiled sheepishly.

"If you had any idea how beautiful you are, how good you taste to me…"

A lot of men had said a lot of things to her over the years. Liam's words blew her mind.

"Come back up here," she said, pulling on his hair to encourage him.

He came willingly. She kissed him deeply, getting turned-on all over again by his apparently unending need for her. She reached between their bodies to find the stud on his jeans, sliding it free and unzipping him without breaking their kiss. He was hard and silky, ready for her. She wanted him inside her, filling her.

She pushed his jeans down to free him and guided his erection between her thighs. The first nudge of his hardness against her made her inner muscles tighten. Then he was sliding into her, thick and long and exactly what she needed.

He stroked into her once, twice, then his fingers gripped her hips and he stilled.

"Zoe—"

She knew what he was worried about.

"I'm safe, I promise," she assured him. She didn't want to be separated from him by a piece of latex. She wanted all of him against all of her.

He hesitated briefly, then he began to move again. He kissed her as his cock stroked her, his whole body hard and focused. He filled her utterly, stretched her, and every thrust sent shivers of reaction through her.

Desire tightened low in her belly for the second time. Liam broke their kiss to press his face into her neck.

"You feel so good, Zoe. So good," he murmured as he peppered kisses on her skin.

"So do you, Liam. You feel perfect."

His hands tightened on her hips and he thrust deeper, harder into her. She met him thrust for thrust, tilting her hips to deepen his penetration. She felt the exact moment when he reached the end of his tether. His body slammed into hers in one final, deep stroke. He pressed his hips into hers, his mouth open on her neck. He exhaled in a rush that almost sounded like a sob. She forgot to breathe as the last shudders of his body tipped her over into her own climax. She tightened around him, milking the last of his orgasm, totally lost to everything but the feel of him in her, around her.

Her heartbeat was still pounding in her ears as Liam's hand found the back of her head. He held her close for what felt like a long time, their bodies still locked together, his face pressed into her neck. She could feel how tense he was, could feel the bulge of his hard bicep against her back. She wished she could see his face, wished she knew what he was thinking.

"Liam?" she finally said.

He lifted his head, then flexed his hips and withdrew from her. She felt the loss, the emptiness that he left behind. He didn't look up as he took a step away from her, concentrating on pulling up his jeans and tucking himself away.

She dropped her own gaze to her knees. Her chest felt impossibly heavy. Just seconds ago they had been one. Now they were two very separate, distant beings. And she still had no idea what Liam felt about her—apart from the fact that, contrary to what she'd initially believed, he found her desirable.

Apparently, that wasn't enough.

Be careful what you wish for, Zoe, she thought mockingly.

She'd wanted to see how far she could push him. That was what the skirt and the shoes and makeup had been all about. Well, now she knew. She could push him into sex. He wanted her. But he didn't want to want her. He resented it, resisted it.

She had a bad taste in her mouth. She recognized it: disappointment. She'd swallowed enough of it over the years to know.

She pushed herself off the table and tugged her skirt down. Her bra dangled from her elbows and she slid the straps back up her arms and hooked it closed. Liam waited until she'd pulled on her underwear before speaking.

"Zoe—"

"Don't say it. I don't want to hear it."

"That shouldn't have happened."

She looked at him, anger searing through the regret and hurt of his withdrawal.

"Don't apologize to me. Don't stand there and tell me how you never meant to touch me, how much you wish you hadn't. It was good. Don't ruin it."

She pushed past him. The guys all pretended to be very involved with their work when she exited the file room and strode toward the door.

She drove home and showered, scrubbing off the makeup,

trying to wash away the red suck marks he'd left on her breasts and thighs.

How could a man want her so much one moment, then barely be able to look at her the next? She didn't understand it. Did he think she wanted a commitment, was that it? Did he think she would put pressure on him, ask for things he wasn't prepared to give?

She shook her head angrily as she dressed. If only he knew. She was in no position to ask anything of him.

Maybe she should tell him, let him know he was off the hook for all the commitments that women usually wanted from men. She was never going to ask him to marry her or have a child with her. She was every red-blooded guy's wet dream—a woman who liked sex and would never, ever make demands. Liam had no idea what a good deal he was turning his back on.

She drove back to the workshop dressed in jeans and a T-shirt, her hair pulled back in a damp ponytail. She'd been gone forty minutes and she didn't look at anyone as she made her way to her workbench.

She kept her shoulders square as she picked up her pencil. It wasn't until she'd been working for ten minutes and Liam still hadn't come to talk to her that she realized she'd been waiting for him to do just that.

Finally, after another ten minutes had passed, she glanced over her shoulder toward his office. The seat behind his desk was empty.

She stared at it for a long moment, then turned back to her work.

Easy come, easy go.

Pity she didn't believe it.

LIAM LEANED LOW over the handlebars of his custom chopper and let the wind rip at his clothes.

He had to find a way to deal with Zoe.

He had to find a way to stop wanting her.

It wasn't until he saw a tall, green line of cypress pines ahead that he realized where his subconscious had led him. He turned the bike into the sedately curved driveway of the Springvale Cemetery and throttled back. He parked in a designated spot and carried his helmet under his arm as he walked across the lawn to the memorial garden where his mother was buried.

A small bronze plaque marked her resting place. The grass was neatly trimmed around it but a few old leaves obscured her name. He squatted and brushed them aside so that he could see her properly. Marianne Louise Masters. Dead at the too-early age of thirty-nine.

She'd had a hard life. Not a lot of money when she was growing up, then she'd fallen pregnant to Graham Masters, her high-school boyfriend, when she was just nineteen. They'd married but she'd lost the baby. Liam had come along a few years later. By then his father had already developed into a problem drinker. He'd always had a volatile temper and with alcohol in the mix it hadn't been long before he started taking his frustrations out on his wife and child. By the time Liam was eight he'd had a broken arm, a perforated eardrum and two separate cases of broken ribs. His mother had fared far worse. A broken jaw. A dislocated shoulder. Lost teeth, blackened eyes. And whatever punishment his father had meted out in the bedroom.

They'd run away twice. Both times his father had hunted them down. They'd left too many clues, trusted the wrong people. The last time they ran, they took only what they could carry and went as far as they could with the money his mother had managed to hide from the weekly budget. All the way from Queensland down the coast of Australia, then across to Adelaide. For the first couple of years they'd moved every few months, just to be safe. They'd wound up in Melbourne when Liam was twelve. The three years they'd spent there had been the best of his young life.

Then his mom had gotten sick.

Liam stood and stared along the green swathe of lawn. A few graves had withered flowers on them, others had plastic posies faded by the harsh Australian sun. His mom had never encouraged flowers. Not when she was sick, and she hadn't wanted them at her funeral.

He pressed a kiss to his fingers and bent to transfer it to the plaque. Then he walked back down the hill.

It had been good to come here. He'd needed to remind himself what was at stake. He'd needed to stare the ugly truth in the eye, absorb it, make it a part of him again.

Because he would never put himself in a situation where he had the opportunity to become his father's son.

In the years after leaving the sanctuary of the Fords' he'd lived hard. He'd drunk a lot, fought a lot, screwed around a lot. Then one day he'd gotten wasted and wound up in a bar fight for no good reason other than that he was drunk and spoiling for a fight and some guy had looked at him funny. He'd woken up the next day and looked in the mirror and seen his father staring back at him. It had chilled him to the bone. From that day on, he'd never been drunk, and he'd never hit a man in anger.

And he'd never let himself get serious with a woman. There was too much of his father in him for him to risk trying for a wife and family of his own. For his mother's sake he would ensure that the cycle of violence ended with him. It was a promise he'd made her long ago, and he'd keep it if it killed him.

Which meant he had to find a way to come to terms with his feelings for Zoe. He would not embark on a relationship with her that would lead nowhere. He'd hurt women in the past with his refusal to commit. Zoe would not be one of them.

He was no closer to having an answer to his dilemma by the time he rode into the parking lot at Masters Mechanics an hour later. Zoe had been under his skin since he was kid. He had no idea how to get her out.

She was working with the airbrush when he walked past her. She didn't look up and he didn't stop to talk to her. There were things that needed to be said, but he couldn't say them right now.

He managed to avoid her for the rest of the day. He was congratulating himself on the fact when a knock sounded on his office door and he looked up to see her standing there.

"You got a minute?" she asked. Her expression was absolutely neutral. He braced himself.

"Sure."

She didn't come right in. Instead, she went to her workbench to collect the Harley fuel tank and her sketch pad. She placed the tank front and center on his desk, slapping the sketch pad down beside it.

"This is what I've come up with," she said.

He studied the intricate image she'd created on the teardrop-shaped fuel tank. A woman's face and torso pushed out from the front like the old-fashioned figurehead on a ship. Wings sprouted from her shoulders and ran down the sides of the tank. Toward the rear, flames licked, a blaze of glory trailing behind her, tangling with her flowing hair. He studied the detail of Zoe's image, picking up on the little visual cues in her work.

"She's like an old sailor's tattoo. Almost a mermaid," he said, slowly getting it. "Old school."

She nodded, arms crossed over her chest. "That's right."

She stood very still, her gaze on his face. Waiting for his verdict.

"It's great," he said.

"You still want me to do the bike, then?"

"Of course. Definitely. This is very, very cool. What did the guys think?"

"They like it. Paul suggested a candied-cherry base coat, more flames on the fenders."

Liam nodded. "Yeah. And let's pick up this orange and purple from her hair."

"Okay. Good. I'll do some more practice runs on the scrap Vinnie found for me while you guys do your bit with fabrication," she said.

She collected the fuel tank and her sketch book and turned to go. He knew it made him the biggest pussy in the world but he was glad that their talk had been all business.

She was almost out the door when he caught the expression on her face. She looked disappointed. Hurt.

Shit.

He was trying to do what he could to protect her, but every time he touched her he made things more confusing. For both of them.

He ran a hand through his hair.

"Zoe, wait."

6

LIAM HAD TO SAY SOMETHING. He'd had sex with her twice, and both times he'd screwed things up. He needed to somehow make her understand that keeping things platonic was the best way to go.

Zoe waited in the doorway, half turned toward him. She held the fuel tank in front of her like a shield.

"What?"

"We need to talk," he said.

She gave him a cool look. "Isn't that my line?"

"You need to understand something. Whatever this is between us, it can't go anywhere. I'm not relationship material. I'm never going to get married or settle down."

He held her gaze even though it was tough to see the way she withdrew into herself more and more with every word he said.

"What happened before and at the club…I shouldn't have lost control. I didn't mean to mislead you," he said.

Zoe raised her eyes to the ceiling as though seeking patience.

"You are one arrogant son of a bitch, you know that?" she said.

He blinked. Not what he'd expected.

"You think that every woman you sleep with wants happy ever after and a white picket fence with you? Think again. In case you hadn't noticed, there were two people in the room every time we got naked. Two people who lost control or whatever you called it. I did what I did with you because I wanted to sleep with you. Nothing more."

"You deserve more than a one-night stand," he said.

"You don't get it, do you? Shock, horror, Liam, but not all of us want to settle down in Pleasantville with you for the rest of eternity. You're a sexy guy with a hot body. That's the sum total of everything I'm interested in."

He shook his head, rejecting her cut-and-dried take on the situation. Whatever was between him and Zoe was about more than sex. They were drawn together. Always had been.

"No," he said.

She frowned. "What is it with you always thinking you know me better than I know myself? I'm not the girl you knew twelve years ago, Liam. I'm all grown up and I know what I want. At the moment, that happens to be sex with you. But that will probably change in a couple of weeks. Usually does." She eyed him steadily. "You don't owe me anything. You don't need to protect me or feel guilty about anything we do together. If you want to sleep with me, all you have to do is say so. That's how easy it is."

She was offering him a free pass, an invitation to sleep with her with no strings attached. He didn't say anything because he didn't know what to say. He wanted her. But he also wanted more than sex. That was the problem.

Zoe hovered in the doorway. When he didn't say anything she shrugged.

"Fine. You know where to find me if you ever decide to stop living in the past. But don't wait too long. I'm not exactly known for my quiet lifestyle."

She left his office, shoulders straight. He swore and kicked his desk.

He was trying to do the right thing by Zoe, by the Fords. It was why he'd left her all those years ago—he'd been trying to save her from himself. Even back then he'd known he was bad for her. But now she was telling him she didn't want to be saved, that she didn't want any of the things he thought she did.

He didn't know what to do. She'd been the great unknown of his life for so long, the perfect, generous girl he'd denied himself because he'd been determined to do the right thing. But Zoe had just told him that she wasn't that perfect girl anymore. He knew she was right—but he also knew in his gut that she was wrong, too. She would always be the perfect girl he fell in love with. But there was no denying that she had grown up and that she was a far different, more daring, more difficult woman than he'd ever imagined.

He wanted to take her up on her offer so much that he literally ached. He wanted to make her come a million different ways. He wanted to swallow her cries and devour her body.

He was in way over his head.

He forced himself to sit behind his desk rather than go after her. He knew himself well enough to know that having a little of what he wanted would be far worse than never having had it at all. Witness his constant awareness of Zoe after only two hard-and-fast encounters. How would he ever walk away from her if he indulged himself fully? Far better not to put himself in such a stupid position in the first place.

He could control things at the moment. Just. As long as he didn't spend too much time alone with her.

He opened his diary, scanning the pages. He could organize a bunch of off-site meetings over the next few weeks, make himself scarce around the place. And there was that trip to Sydney he'd been putting off. If he worked at it, he could find plenty of ways to make sure temptation never drew him into Zoe's arms again.

He was settled in his own mind that that was the best course of action. Yet somehow when he drove home that night, he found himself standing in front of Zoe's portrait. He'd unwrapped it a few nights ago and he stood staring at her a long time. Then he grabbed the painting and walked it through to the garage, where he covered it with a drop cloth.

Enough. No more temptation. He'd never been a masochist, and he wasn't about to start now.

LUCKY LICKED ZOE'S HAND affectionately when she picked the cat up from the vet clinic later that night. She lay curled in the bottom of the expensive pet carrier Zoe had bought, her four kittens snugged against her belly. Zoe kept glancing at the tiny, fuzzy little kittens as she drove home, delighted by their small squashed faces and determinedly closed eyes. They would need to stay with Lucky for at least six weeks to make sure they got all the nutrients they needed, but after that Zoe would have to find them homes. Even at her most optimistic, she couldn't imagine herself being able to comfortably house five cats in her tiny studio.

For the first time in a long time her apartment felt like home as she settled mother and babies into "their" corner. She'd splashed out on a basket and various cat toys as well as the carrier, and she spent nearly an hour lying on her belly, stroking Lucky and the kittens, inhaling their soft, warm smell.

Despite herself, her thoughts kept drifting to Liam, to what he'd said and what she'd said to him in return. She didn't understand why he was holding back—especially now she'd let him know there would never be any strings attached to any physical relationship they might have. She was a past master of the casual fling—sex for as long as it felt good and stayed fun. She knew absolutely that she and Liam could have a lot of fun together if he let them. But he wasn't interested, apparently. Despite how good the sex was.

Useless to pretend that his rejection didn't sting. It wasn't the first time he'd kept her at arm's length. Question was, when was she going to learn where he was concerned?

Satisfied the cats were safe and warm, Zoe finally put herself to bed. She got up twice during the night to make sure they were doing okay, then found herself anguishing about leaving them at home on their own when she went to work. It was a Saturday and technically she didn't have to be there but she knew Liam and most of the guys were pulling overtime to finish bikes and get them out of the way so they could concentrate on the competition chopper.

After a few minutes of indecision the following morning she packed Lucky and her kittens into the pet carrier again. All they did at the moment was eat and sleep; they wouldn't be a problem if she kept them beside her workbench.

To her surprise, she'd no sooner put the carrier down than she had a crowd of big, tough guys gathered around taking turns to stroke small furry bodies and suggest names for Lucky's children. She'd rejected Bruiser, Snoozer, Loser and Cruiser along with a host of other equally inappropriate names by the time she felt the instinctive prickle on the back of her neck that told her Liam had arrived.

She glanced up from her position kneeling beside the carrier to find him standing there, arms crossed over his chest.

"They won't be a problem, I promise," she said quickly. "Lucky just sleeps all day and the kittens haven't even opened their eyes yet."

"Although Bruiser there is definitely making an effort," Vinnie said. He'd already put his hand up for the little black and white kitten.

Liam still didn't say anything. The guys exchanged glances

and drifted to their work stations. Zoe stood and smoothed her hands down the thighs of her jeans.

"Look, if it's going to be a problem just say so," she said.

"I was thinking they might be warmer in my office," Liam said. "There's a bit of a draft through here."

She opened her mouth to say something, then realized she didn't know what to say.

She finally opted for "Thanks."

He shrugged one big shoulder and leaned down to pick up the carrier. She followed him to his office and crouched down to arrange Lucky's water bowl in front of the carrier as he settled it in the corner.

"You're right, it's definitely warmer in here," she said. Suddenly she felt awkward around him. Which was stupid. They'd cleared the air yesterday, hadn't they? She'd made an offer, he'd rejected it. In doing so, they'd established their relationship was all about work and nothing else.

"Yeah."

She was fussing unnecessarily with Lucky's blanket and she pushed herself to her feet.

"Better get back to it," she said. "I hear the boss is a real hard-ass."

He rewarded her small joke with a half smile. She searched his face, trying to interpret his mood. He seemed…withdrawn. Reserved. She dropped her gaze. This was probably the way it was going to be between them from now on— friendly but professional. Distant.

She returned to her workbench and started setting up her airbrush for the day's work. She concentrated fiercely on the job at hand. Anything to avoid thinking or feeling. She knew from long experience that she could bury almost anything if she tried hard enough.

By lunchtime she'd found homes for all but one of the

kittens. Apparently she wasn't the only one who was a sucker for soft fur and squashed faces. Liam went out just before lunch and she took the opportunity to spend her own break with Lucky in his office, sitting cross-legged beside the carrier and petting Lucky until she purred.

Zoe was cuddling a squirming kitten in her hand, laughing at the tiny pinprick of its claws, when a shadow fell over her. Liam, back from lunch.

"Sorry. I'll get out of your hair," she said. From where she was sitting on the floor, he looked very big and broad.

"No rush. No need to disturb the little guy."

He crouched beside her and reached out to run a finger down the kitten's spine.

"This one got a name yet?" he asked.

"Not really. Vinnie wanted to call him Loser because he's the smallest, but there's no way I'm sending a kitten out into the world with a name like that."

Liam stroked the kitten again and it lifted its blind face and nuzzled his fingers.

"Do you want to hold him?" she asked.

Before he could say no, she transferred the kitten to his palm.

He winced as the kitten kneaded his thumb pad with its needle-sharp claws, obviously looking for food.

"I know. Kind of like getting a tattoo, don't you think?" She laughed.

"Yeah, only there's no payoff at the end of the pain." He lifted the kitten closer to his face. "Little dude, listen up. Here's your first lesson in life—thumbs do not produce milk. Okay?"

There was something about the sight of the tiny, defenseless kitten curled in the palm of his big, work-hardened hand that made her stomach twist.

She studied him from beneath her eyelashes, fascinated by the contrast between the size and strength of his powerful body and the gentleness of his touch as he held the kitten.

"You found homes for them all yet?" he asked.

"All except for Little Dude here," she said.

He shot her a dry look.

"Nice try, but I'm a dog man," he said.

She shrugged a shoulder. "Suit yourself."

He gently placed the kitten with his mother.

"How's the design coming along?" he asked.

"Good. I've been working on some flames, using the purple with the red and orange like you suggested. I think it's going to work really well."

"Excellent."

They stood at the same time.

"Well," she said, apropos of nothing.

She stepped around him and left his office. It was only when she went to pick up her air gun that she realized how much her hands were shaking.

Damn.

She closed her eyes for a second.

Time to be honest with yourself, Zoe.

She liked him way too much. And it wasn't just a sex thing. She wanted to jump him, yes. But she wanted to make him laugh, and she wanted to talk to him and she wanted to know and understand him.

All stupid, dangerous indulgences for someone like herself. Just as well Liam had said no to her little offer yesterday.

She opened her eyes and reached for her work. She was almost through her first week. Only three more to go.

Bring it on.

HE'D BEEN DOING really well until lunchtime. Then he'd caught Zoe in his office doting on her cats and all the resolve in him just…dissolved.

Hard-ass Zoe he could withstand. She traded on sex and temptation and he could resist her. Barely. It was simply a matter of self-control.

But when Zoe let her guard down, when she looked at him with no wariness in her eyes and he saw her younger self staring back at him—well, he was lost. She made him remember the way it used to be.

All night he'd sweated her offer. What man wouldn't? She was gorgeous, incredibly desirable. She was offering herself to him on a platter. And—as he'd already established several times—he was not a saint.

The afternoon was a write-off workwise. He kept telling himself to leave, to find some business to take care of off-site. But he couldn't make himself leave her orbit.

Then there were the damned kittens. Three times he had to get up to see why they were mewling so much. The first time it was a territorial dispute, with Little Dude being pushed aside by a bigger, tougher sister. The second time the water bowl needed refilling. The third time it was Little Dude again, in distress for no good reason that Liam could see. He picked the damned fur ball up and cradled it against his chest for a few minutes and that seemed to calm the kitten. He was repositioning him amongst his brothers and sisters again when he glanced toward the doorway and saw Zoe there, watching him.

"He was complaining, making a fuss," he said.

"He's probably hungry. They're always hungry," she said. "And he's got a bit of catching up to do."

"Yeah."

She was watching him, an amused light in her eyes. God, he wanted to kiss her. His staff could all go to hell as far as he was concerned—he wanted to kiss her and haul her onto his desk and bury himself inside her and hang the consequences.

"Thanks for looking after him, anyway," she said.

"You should go," he said suddenly. "Home, I mean. Most of the guys are about to call it quits. You've already worked most of your Saturday."

"Are you sure?" she asked. "I want to pull my own weight."

"Absolutely. The competition bike's more than on track."

"Okay, then. Thanks. I'll just clear away my gear then come get Lucky."

He let his breath out when she left his office. Good. Temptation removed for another day. Tomorrow was Sunday, which meant a whole day of blessed relief, then the torture would begin for another week.

She was back in five minutes, her jacket on and car keys in hand.

He helped her pack away the water bowl and insisted on hefting the carrier for her, even though it wasn't heavy.

It didn't escape him that he was literally escorting her from the premises.

She took the carrier from him when they got to the car. He should have gone inside and left her to it, but instead he watched as she used the seat belt to strap the carrier into the backseat and fussed to make sure mother and babies were all comfortable for the journey home. He studied her profile, then the long line of her legs, then, finally, the firm curves of her ass. Her T-shirt had pulled loose from her waistband at the small of her back and he stared at the smooth, creamy skin on display. His hands curled of their own volition and he shoved them into his back pockets to stop himself from touching her.

She was smiling indulgently when she backed out of the car.

"It's going to be hard to give those little guys up," she said.

She reached behind herself to tuck herself in, and her T-shirt tightened across her breasts. He stared, unable to help himself.

"God, Zoe," he groaned. "Just go, already. Please."

Her startled gaze found his. One glance at his crotch was enough to give the game away. A knowing look came into her eyes.

"I'll be back next week, you know, Liam."

"I know."

"And for another two weeks after that."

"Yep. I remember."

Her gaze dropped to his crotch again. She wet her bottom lip.

"You going to send me home early every day?"

"Maybe. Probably."

She nodded, then looked him very directly in the eyes.

"Your choice. It's a free country."

She selected her ignition key from her key ring and turned away, reaching for the car door.

She'd been in his head for years. He'd been fooling himself when he thought he could keep his distance.

"Wait," he said.

She stilled, her back to him. His arms slid around her, pulling her back against his chest. One of his hands found her hip while the other came to rest just beneath her breasts. He leaned forward and pressed his face into the nape of her neck, inhaling deeply.

She smelled good. Right. Perfect.

He could feel her heart pounding against her rib cage. His was going crazy, too.

"Come back to my place," he said.

He felt her breath leave her in a rush.

"Yes."

"Give me a minute to grab my gear," he said.

He realized some of the guys had been watching them when he strode back toward his office to grab his keys and jacket. He didn't give a damn.

He wanted Zoe. He felt like he'd wanted her all his life. He was sick of fighting it. Tonight, she would be his. Tomorrow… He'd worry about tomorrow when the time came.

ZOE COULD FEEL her pulse pounding in her neck. She was going home with Liam. She still couldn't quite believe it. She shifted in her seat as she accelerated away from an intersection, remembering the way his arms had slid around her, the gravel in his voice when he asked her to come home with him.

No more games. No more pretense. No more denial.

Up ahead she saw the signal on his chopper flash for a left turn. She followed him into a broad, leafy street, one of St. Kilda's finest. Big, expensive houses marched down either side of the road. Surely he didn't live around here?

Her stomach dipped when he turned into the driveway of a large, modern home. She reminded herself that Liam was a very successful man. Somehow she kept getting him tangled up in her mind with the young man she'd known all those years ago.

Made from a mix of wood, masonry and glass, the house in front of her was contemporary in style and boasted two levels and a triple garage. She couldn't help smiling as the garage door lifted to reveal Liam's vintage Mustang, a large black SUV and another three motorbikes in addition to the chopper he was riding.

Boys and their toys.

Liam had already parked his bike and was stripping off his helmet and leather jacket as she pulled up. He waited for her to turn the engine off before opening the rear door of the car and grabbing the cat carrier. She wondered how many of his girlfriends came complete with traveling pet nurseries, then quickly pushed the thought from her mind. It didn't matter. For starters, she wasn't his girlfriend. She was simply some-one he was attracted to, someone he was going to sleep with. As such, she had no business wondering about the other women in his life. Whoever they might be.

"We'll go in through the garage. It's easier," he said.

As she followed him inside, the smell of fresh paint hit her.

"Have you been renovating?" she asked.

They were walking down a hallway with high ceilings and unadorned off-white walls.

"Building. The original house on this site was falling over when I bought it. I bulldozed it and had this place built."

Her jaw went a little slack as she followed him into a large, open living space. Huge cathedral ceilings, lots of light, more neutral paint and more blank walls. The only color came from the golden hardwood floor and the dark slate of the fire-place surround. He had the bare minimum of furniture—a man-size couch in brown leather and a huge flat-screen TV and precious little else.

"How long have you been living here?"

"Four months."

And he still hadn't furnished the place?

He kept walking, leading her into a big, modern kitchen fitted with light wood units and cream Corian countertops.

"Wow. This is huge," she said.

He had an ice-making fridge and a superwide oven, the kind that looked like it belonged in a restaurant.

He shrugged, almost as though he was a little embarrassed.

"It's a kitchen. It gets the job done."

He put the cat carrier down, then refilled the water bowl.

Zoe stood and watched him, her thumbs hooked into the front pockets of her jeans.

Her shoulders were tight, her belly tense. She was nervous. Which was nuts. It wasn't like she'd never had sex before. But this was Liam's place, his territory. And she wasn't armed with any of her usual defenses. No fishnet stockings, no makeup, no stilettos. It was just her and Liam.

He crossed to the sink and washed his hands. She watched as he dried them carefully on a tea towel. His dark eyes held hers as he put the towel down and walked toward her. She expected him to stop before he was within touching distance, but he didn't. He stepped right up to her, so close that her breasts brushed his chest and she could feel the heat radiating off his body.

"Zoe Ford. What am I going to do with you?" he asked in a low, low tone.

She was having trouble breathing as she looked into his eyes. "I have a few ideas."

"Yeah?"

He tucked a strand of hair behind her ear. His fingers trailed down her neck until his hand landed warm and heavy on her shoulder.

"Like what?"

The look in his eyes…

"We could—" She broke off in frustration and shook her head. She slid a hand behind his neck, standing on tiptoe as she drew him down to her. His lips were firm and warm against hers and she traced them with her tongue before sliding inside to explore him more fully. His tongue slid along hers and a shiver of need raced up her spine.

He pulled back. Already his chest was rising and falling like he'd just run a mile. She loved that she affected him so profoundly.

"Let's go for broke and try to make it to a bedroom this time. What do you say?" he said.

"Sounds like a plan."

He grabbed her hand and led her into the living room, then up a wide flight of stone and wrought-iron stairs. He pulled her into the first doorway and she got a vague impression of an unmade bed, a pile of clothes in the corner and more neutral colors before Liam was tugging her back into his arms.

His kiss was so urgent, so hungry that it took what was left of her breath away. He toed off his boots and she followed suit, never breaking their kiss. He tugged her T-shirt free from her jeans and dragged it over her head. His pupils dilated as he stared at her breasts, spilling out of red lace.

"Zoe. Man, if you only knew how much I love red lace," he said.

She reached for his T-shirt, pulling it over his head and letting it fall to the ground. He had a great chest, so wide and strong. She eyed it avidly, remembering the long hours she'd had to keep her hands off him when she gave him the tattoo sitting low on his belly.

Not anymore.

She reached out and slid her hands over his hard, round pecs. She raked her fingernails against his skin. He was so big, all man. She wanted to bite him and lick him and taste him all over.

She pushed him backward until the bed hit the back of his knees. She found the stud on his jeans and had it undone in seconds, his fly moments after that. She grabbed a fistful of denim on either side of his hips and tugged his jeans and boxer-briefs down at the same time. His erection sprang free, big and thick and proud. He stepped out of his clothes and she couldn't help herself. She dropped to her knees, pushing her face against him and inhaling the smell of him, spicy and male. She traced the base of his erect shaft with her tongue, feeling him shudder in response. Then she slid her tongue along his length until she found his swollen, velvet head.

"Zoe," he said.

She took him into her mouth, all of him, savoring the length and heft of him. He was beautiful. She couldn't wait to have him inside her.

She sucked him hard, then rubbed the rough of her tongue across the head of his erection. He groaned and his hands slid into her hair. She smiled around him, enjoying the power, turned-on by how aroused he was.

She took him deep into her mouth again and again, teasing him with her tongue, using her hand to stroke his shaft. She felt his body growing more and more tense. Finally she pushed him back onto the bed. He lay there, his feet still on the floor, knees bent over the edge of the bed, his cock wet and hard from her mouth.

She shucked her jeans and underwear in record time and dispensed with her bra with a deft flick of her wrist. Then she climbed on top of him, straddling his hips.

She grasped his erection in her hand and guided it between her legs, sliding his plump head into her wetness so he would know how turned-on she was. His eyes were half-closed, his mouth slightly open as he watched her. She rocked forward, rubbing her breasts against his chest, loving the crispness of his chest hair against her sensitive flesh. He pulled her higher still and sucked an already taut nipple into his mouth, his tongue hot and fast against her.

Suddenly she was desperate for him. With a tilt of her hips, she had him in position. Slowly she bore down.

He was hard and thick and he felt so good she stilled, her fingers clutching at his arms as she savored the stretch of her body, the heat of his.

Her eyes tightly closed, she concentrated on the sensation of fullness, completeness.

She started to move, circling her hips as she slid up his shaft then down again, each delicious stroke making her ache for ten more. His hands replaced his mouth on her breasts, plucking at her nipples, rolling them between his fingers, pinching her.

She bit her lip and increased her pace, chasing the tension inside herself. She breathed in the smell of sex and Liam and desire and felt her climax begin to take her.

"Not yet, baby," he said. He shifted beneath her so quickly that before she knew it she was on her back and he was on top of her, his weight bearing her down into the mattress.

He kissed her deeply, his forearms planted either side of her shoulders, his hips thrusting into her.

He slid a hand down her thigh to her knee and lifted it higher, slipping it over his shoulder. Then he was deeper inside her, pounding into her. They stared into each other's eyes, both gasping for breath, lost in desire.

Her climax hit her and she cried out. She grasped his hips and ass and held him to her as she shuddered around him, her neck arched back, her eyes clenched shut. He stepped up his pace, his thrusts almost desperate. She opened her eyes in time to see him come, teeth bared, face tight.

He withdrew and rolled onto his back. They were both sticky with sweat and breathing hard. The sensitive flesh between her legs throbbed with satisfaction. She could feel the hairiness of his calf against hers, smell the citrus tang of his aftershave.

"Say something," he said after a long silence.

She turned her head to look at him.

"Wow."

The corners of his mouth tilted up into a smile. Then his

gaze dipped below her face to scan her breasts and her belly, finally focusing on her mound.

"You have to be anywhere tonight?" he asked, his gaze never leaving her thighs.

"No."

"Want to stay for dinner?"

"What are we having?"

He met her eyes and grinned.

"You."

She laughed.

"Is there dessert, too?" she asked.

But he wasn't smiling anymore. His focus had shifted to her belly. To her tattoo, to be exact. Everything inside her went cold as he reached out to trace the neat line of her scar where it ran across the top of her pubic bone. They made them a lot smaller these days but her surgery had been an emergency procedure and the line was nearly seven inches long. Only the expert shading of her tattoo had hidden it from him until now.

"What's this?" he asked.

Tell him. Tell him and get it out of the way.

She opened her mouth, but no words came out. She didn't want to see his eyes fill with pity. She didn't want him to look at her and see nothing but an empty vessel. Liam had known her before. For some reason, that meant something.

"Nothing," she said.

She'd hesitated too long. He frowned.

"It's a freaking great scar, Zoe. It's not nothing," he said.

"I had appendicitis," she lied.

He rolled onto his back and patted his belly. Too late she saw the thin white line of an old appendix scar. "Nope. Try again."

He was watching her, waiting for her to lay herself out in

front of him. The thought of telling him made bile rise up the back of her throat.

So maybe she wasn't as resigned to her fate as she'd convinced herself she was. Something she could deal with later, when she wasn't being asked to bare her soul.

"Ever think that maybe I don't want to tell you because maybe it's none of your business?"

His gaze remained steady.

"Tell me what happened, Zoe," he said quietly.

She pushed herself up onto her elbows and wriggled to the edge of the bed.

"Where are you going?" he asked.

"Home, where nobody hassles me." She reached for her clothes, but Liam was suddenly on his feet, kicking them away from her.

She tried to get past him but he grabbed her and pushed her back onto the bed. Before she could recover he was on top of her, his superior weight and strength pinning her to the mattress.

"I might just be a glorified grease monkey, but I know this is important. Talk to me, Zoe."

She glared at him. He wasn't going to give up. She pushed at his shoulders.

"Get off me," she said.

"I knew a woman once who had a scar like that," he said, his gaze holding hers. "She'd had a cesarean. Did you have a baby, Zoe? Is that what happened?"

God, the irony. His guess was almost funny. Almost.

"Get. Off. Me."

Slowly he rolled to one side. She stared at the ceiling and took a deep breath.

"You want to know what happened? Fine. I had an ectopic pregnancy. I lost my right ovary and my uterus. I can't ever have children. Happy now?"

7

ZOE'S WORDS HUNG in the air. Liam didn't know what to do, what to say. He didn't know what he'd expected her to reveal, but not this.

"Jesus. I'm sorry, Zoe."

She shrugged a shoulder. "It was a long time ago."

Like it was no big deal.

"Some things never get easier."

She didn't take her eyes off the ceiling. "It is what it is. No point getting all cut up over something that's never going to be any different."

Her jaw was clenched, her hands curled into fists.

"You're allowed to be pissed off," he said.

"Like I said, it was so long ago, I can't remember things being any different."

He frowned. That was the second time she'd referred to her pregnancy happening some time ago.

"How old were you?"

"Nearly sixteen. Just another stupid drunk kid at a party doing stupid drunk things."

Nearly sixteen. She'd gotten pregnant right after he'd left. Tom's words from the other day flashed across his mind. *She took your leaving hard. Really hard.*

He swore and sat up. There was no way the timing was a coincidence.

"Jesus Christ," he said, dragging both hands through his hair.

The Zoe he'd known back then would never have gotten drunk at a party. He knew exactly the kind of demons that drove kids to drink to excess, and she hadn't had it in her.

Not until he'd come into her life.

"It happens every day," she said. "Kids get carried away, don't think about the consequences. I'm a walking cautionary tale."

He looked at her. He knew the truth.

"It wouldn't have happened if I'd been around."

"You're psychic now, are you?" she asked.

"It wouldn't have happened."

She broke eye contact and shrugged. "I was just unlucky, that's all. Maybe if Marty Johannsen hadn't walked me home—"

"Marty Johannsen!"

Marty was a weak bully and exactly the kind of sleazy prick who'd take advantage of Zoe when she was drunk. The thought of him being her first, of him pushing himself inside her and destroying all her sweetness made Liam want to hurt something.

"Tell me Tom beat the shit out of him afterward," he asked grimly. "Tell me he rearranged his face."

"It wasn't rape, Liam. I knew exactly what I was doing."

He swore again and paced to the bedroom door and back again. He understood what she was saying. She'd slept with Marty to forget him, to get over him. Because he'd walked out on her, refused to take what she'd so generously, innocently offered.

Life's great irony: he'd left to save her from himself and she'd thrown herself away on a dumb asshole who hadn't cared enough to protect her.

Zoe stood and began collecting her clothes.

"You wanted to know. That's the only reason I told you. It's my business, nobody else's," she said. She held her bundled clothes against her belly.

"That's bullshit and you know it," he said, glaring at her. "This is my business. This is absolutely my business."

"No, Liam, it isn't. You weren't there."

She walked out the door without another word. He was so angry he doubled his hand into a fist and slammed it into the wall. Plaster gave and the wall shook. He stared at the hole he'd made and forced himself to take deep breaths down into his belly.

A minute later he heard Zoe's car start up in the driveway.

He didn't know where to put himself. He was furious, the discipline of years the only thing keeping him from losing it completely. He pushed his feet into his gym shoes and pulled on underwear, a pair of shorts and a tank. He grabbed his boxing gloves and jogged the short distance to the local gym.

He sweated it out on the long bag for over an hour, throwing punches until his shoulders and chest burned and his legs ached. No one approached him or said a word. Finally he let his fists fall to his sides. His breathing was ragged, his clothes plastered to him with sweat. He sank down onto a nearby bench and drank deeply from his water bottle.

His anger was gone, burned out. All he had left was heavy regret and bone-deep sympathy for Zoe. She'd made one mistake, one choice, and it had changed her life. Whether she wanted to admit it or not, he was part of that decision. He knew in his gut that there was no way she would have thrown herself away on a guy like Marty Johannsen if Liam hadn't hurt her. And he would have to live with that knowledge, just as Zoe lived with the scar on her belly and the reality of her inability to have children.

He remembered what she'd said to him in his office yesterday afternoon: *I'm not the girl you knew twelve years ago.*

Now that he could see straight, he wanted to go to her and hold her and say all the reassuring things he should have said when she told him her secret. He wanted to tell her she was beautiful and brave. He wanted to tell her that she was worth so much more than the price she put on herself. He wanted to tell her that she was special and amazing and that she always had been—and that nothing would ever change that, no matter what she thought or believed.

But he couldn't. Now, more than ever, he had to keep his distance. She was a woman who needed to be adored, nurtured, cherished, a woman who needed to understand exactly how loved she was. And he was a man who could only offer a few nights of sex and nothing more. He was only going to hurt her and mess himself up if he kept giving in to the need to be with her.

His jaw set, Liam left the gym and slowly walked home. He had a shower then spent a restless hour watching the weekend football highlights. He didn't give a toss who had won or who was looking good to make the finals.

He couldn't shake the image of Zoe sitting at home alone in her apartment, brooding over what had happened between them today. He couldn't forget the dead, flat sound of her voice as she matter-of-factly told him about what had happened to her.

Out of desperation, he picked up the phone. He called Jacinta and set up a time to see her the next evening. Then he called Tom Ford for the second time in a week.

Zoe was going to be angry when she found out, but she couldn't stop him from helping her. It was either this, or give in to the urge to find her and hold her and be a part of her life.

In other words, no choice. But he'd never had a lot of choices where Zoe was concerned.

ZOE WAS TEMPTED to get wasted again that night. But it hadn't escaped her attention that alcohol had become her refuge of choice over the past week or so. She knew from past experience that she was only setting herself up for an almighty fall if she kept numbing herself with vodka and bourbon.

Hands clasped tightly around her knees, she sat in the middle of her bed and tried to think of something other than drink to help get rid of the ache in her chest.

This was why she hadn't wanted to tell Liam her secret. No good ever came of dredging up the past, talking about stuff that was done and dusted.

And now he knew. Every time he looked at her, he would think about what had happened, about her scar, about her…emptiness. It would always be there between them.

She wished she could forget the look on his face when he'd understood what had happened and who it had happened with. He'd been so angry. She'd felt it radiating off him like heat. Useless to pretend some of that anger hadn't been for her. She'd made a stupid choice. And, yes, she'd suffered the consequences. But the fact remained, she'd chosen to lie down with Marty Johannsen. Everything else had spun out from that one foolish, reckless choice.

Of course Liam was angry with her. Why wouldn't he be? She'd been angry with herself for years.

One thing was for sure—their fling was over before it had ever really started. Which was just as well. She'd kidded herself that it was only about sex, that the heat between her and Liam was all desire and unrequited lust. There was too much of the past mixed up in her attraction to him. It would be very easy to let herself start to believe in something that would never be.

She knew exactly how much she had to offer a man—not enough. Certainly not enough for a man like Liam, a man who had the world at his feet. He might say he wasn't interested in a relationship, that he wasn't "good relationship material" but he wasn't even thirty yet. He'd change. They all did. And when he did decide to commit to someone, it wouldn't be to a messed-up, angry, half woman who brought nothing to the table except a tattoo gun and a stray cat.

But what was new about that? Every serious adult relationship she'd had had foundered on her inability to have children. She'd learned that it was only when the option to have children wasn't there that most men understood how important it was to them. They might not want kids tomorrow, they might not even want them at all, but they wanted the choice to be theirs, not a foregone conclusion.

But the really stupid, stupid thing was that despite knowing the score, despite telling herself that she'd been playing with fire every time she slept with Liam and that it was just sex at the end of the day, just body parts bumping in the night, her chest still ached with loss and misplaced grief.

What did she have to grieve, for Pete's sake? An almost fling with an old crush? It meant nothing, less than nothing.

Sick of herself, she went to bed early and tossed and turned all night. She woke feeling gritty-eyed and exhausted. It wasn't until she was in the shower that she remembered her brother's message from earlier in the week.

She'd never actually got around to returning Tom's phone call to discuss his invitation to lunch today. No accident there. If she didn't call, she wasn't committed either way.

But as she shampooed her hair, she was hit with a sudden, piercing desire to be surrounded by family. Her brother infuriated her at times with his misguided attempts to help her, but he loved her and she loved him. And Jane was a gem, the kind of woman she would have chosen for her brother if she'd been asked to go wife shopping for him. Then there were the kids—Danny, Caleb and Rachel. Zoe smiled as she remembered the elaborate handshake they'd invented between them the last time she'd visited: their secret, aunty shake, a special greeting reserved just for her.

She would go. She'd been foolish to stay away for so long. Pride had played a part. And—if she was being honest—fear. She'd already screwed up so much of her life, she didn't want to lose her brother. Equally, she refused to give up the things that made her who she was. Her tattooing, the band. Somehow Tom was going to have to come to terms with that if they were going to see each other more than once or twice a year.

She dressed in her least-provocative jeans, boots and T-shirt and went next door to ask her elderly neighbour, Nola, if she would mind keeping an eye on Lucky and the kittens. Then she hit the road.

Her stomach danced with nerves as she turned onto the leafy, gracious Hawthorn Street where her brother and his family lived. She should have called to confirm she was coming. Of course she should have. Tom would just assume she wasn't, since she hadn't responded to his message. She'd effectively be turning up on his doorstep unannounced and unexpected.

Zoe made a frustrated noise in the back of her throat, annoyed with her own dithering.

This was her brother. He could deal with a semiunexpected visit from his sister.

She found a parking spot on the street and made her way up the front path. The doorbell echoed loudly in the house and she heard the thump of little feet running up the hallway. Then Rachel was squealing with delight as she opened the door.

"Aunty Zoe, Aunty Zoe!" she said in her high little girl's voice, jumping up and down with excitement. She began struggling with the lock on the security door, standing on tip-toes to reach it. Through the security mesh Zoe could see she was wearing a fairy outfit, complete with wings. Zoe's heart squeezed in her chest.

"Hey, sweetheart. Don't you look pretty," she said.

"Wait up, honey." Her brother's voice came from down the hallway. "You know you're supposed to wait for one of us to open the door with you."

"But it's Aunty Zoe!" Rachel said, as if that excused all sins.

Tom reached the door and she saw the surprise in his eyes as he registered that his wayward sister really was standing on the doorstep.

"Zoe," he said. He shook his head as if to clear it, then flicked the door open and held it wide. "God. It's good to see you. We didn't think you were coming."

He stepped forward and hauled her into his arms, squeezing her tight. Zoe squeezed him back, resting her cheek on his shoulder.

"Sorry," she said. "I was going to call. I just never got around to it."

"Forget it. It's good to see you."

They stepped back from their embrace and eyed each other. He'd put on a little weight, she noticed. He looked happy. She wondered what changes he saw in her.

"Come on in," he said. "I was just about to fire up the barbecue. As usual, Jane has enough food to feed a small army. She must have sensed something."

He was leading her to the family room at the back of the house.

"She'll be in heaven—two extra mouths to feed," he said.

Zoe frowned. Did Tom mean she wasn't the only guest? She'd kind of been counting on this being a private reunion.

Then her step faltered as she entered the living room and saw the broad-shouldered figure leaning casually against the kitchen counter. Liam's dark gaze seemed to pin her from across the room.

"What are you doing here?" she asked rudely.

8

LIAM TOSSED A NUT into his mouth and crunched down on it, supremely at his ease.

"Visiting. Same as you," he said.

Her brother's hand landed on the small of her back and urged her forward, almost as though he understood that her first impulse upon seeing Liam was to turn tail and run.

"Zoe. It's so good to see you. Wow, your hair has grown so long," Jane said, rounding the counter to embrace Zoe.

Tom moved to the back door and hollered into the yard.

"Guys, guess who's come to visit?"

Zoe tore her gaze from Liam's unreadable face as her nephews came barreling into the house. She could feel Liam watching her as she greeted her two nephews.

"I thought you'd forgotten us," Caleb said as he pressed a wet kiss to her cheek.

"No way, José. I've just been busy."

"That's what Daddy said, too," Danny said. "I don't like it when you're too busy for us."

Zoe bit her lip and gave them both an extra squeeze. She was such an idiot for absenting herself from their lives. She made a silent vow to never do it again. She'd missed out on three months of growth and development—Caleb was taller, Danny had lost two teeth and Rachel had clearly discovered her mother's makeup bag in the time since Zoe had last seen them. All things she would have known if she hadn't been so stubborn and stupid.

"I promise it won't happen again," she said as she straightened. "Okay?"

"Deal," Caleb said.

"Double deal," Danny added.

She had to shake both their hands, trying to remember all the ins and outs of their special handshake, then Rachel wanted in on the act. Liam was still watching her when she glanced across at him.

"Someone's popular," he said.

"Zoe's always been great with them," Jane said. "Can I get you a drink, Zoe? Wine, a beer?"

Zoe noted that Liam was drinking a beer. He looked very comfortable in her brother's kitchen. Like hanging out with her family was an everyday occurrence.

She shook her head.

"No, thanks."

She was rattled, no denying it. She hadn't expected to see Liam until tomorrow. She certainly hadn't expected to see him here, deep in her territory. Every time she looked at him she remembered how they'd fallen onto his bed yesterday afternoon, the way they'd savored each other. And the way it had all soured so quickly once he insisted on knowing the truth.

She turned away from him, unable to deal with her own conflicting thoughts and feelings.

"What can I do to help?" she asked her sister-in-law.

Ten minutes later she was up to her elbows in salad ingredients. As she transferred shredded lettuce to a bowl, she glanced out through the French doors to the patio, where Tom and Liam were talking around the barbecue. Liam had his back to her and she eyed his shoulders, hugged by a snug black T-shirt. Had he and Tom decided to renew their friendship after all these years? Was that what this was all about? Was she going to have to get used to finding Liam at family gatherings?

The thought made her stomach twist. She needed less contact with Liam, not more.

"I was so pleased when Tom told me Liam had called," Jane confided as she added sliced tomatoes to the salad. "Tom has always felt so guilty about the way things ended between them."

Zoe concentrated on dicing an onion very finely.

"It's such a coincidence that you and Liam ran into each other at your tattoo parlor," Jane said. "What are the odds, do you think?"

Jane shook her head, clearly amazed by the apparently chance meeting. Zoe shot Liam's back another look. So he hadn't told Tom about the painting, then? How noble of him.

"Yeah. I was pretty surprised," Zoe said, mostly because Jane would expect some kind of response.

"I bet," Jane said. Then she laughed a little self-consciously. "I can understand why you had a crush on him when you were a kid, Zoe. He's a whole hunk of man, isn't he? I bet he has to beat women off with a stick."

"Nothing's going on between us," Zoe said quickly. "He offered me a job, that's all. For old times' sake."

Jane's blue eyes widened and a smile curved her mouth. Zoe bit her lip. She might as well have had T-shirts made. Why on earth had she leaped to defend herself against an insinuation her sister-in-law hadn't even made?

"Well. The job sounds really interesting," Jane said. "I can't wait to see what you come up with. You know how much I love your art."

Jane was the one who had suggested Zoe create some pieces for Tom's office when he was promoted last year. They'd even tried to pay her for them, something Zoe had resisted fiercely.

"Meat's ready," Tom called from outside.

"Okay. Won't be a second," Jane said.

They worked together to finish the salad, and within a couple of minutes they were all settling around the patio table. Zoe wound up sharing a bench seat with Liam. She wasn't quite sure how it happened and she was acutely aware of his body heat, the press of his thigh alongside hers, the brush of his big bicep against her arm as he reached for the salad or passed the tray of burgers and sausages along.

"Liam says he'll cut me a good deal if I want to invest in a custom chopper," Tom said as they all dug into their food.

Jane's knife and fork stilled over her food as she gave her husband a dry look.

"Invest? As in, one day we'll see a return on our money?"

Tom had the good grace to look a little sheepish.

"Each bike is individually handcrafted," he said.

Liam laughed.

"Good luck selling that one," Zoe said to her brother.

"Why do I suddenly feel like the heavy here?" Jane asked.

"Don't. Everyone at this table knows that a custom chopper is a big-boy's toy and that Tom has better uses for his money," Zoe said.

Liam nudged her with his elbow.

"Easy there, champ. That's my livelihood you're talking about. Yours, too, now that I come to think about it."

She propped her elbow on the table and turned to look him full in the eye.

"So you think Tom should buy one of your bikes instead of, say, taking the kids on a trip to Disneyland?" she asked.

Caleb and Danny sat up straight, eyes bugging out of their heads.

"Disneyland?!" they said in unison.

Jane groaned and Tom rolled his eyes.

"Thank you, Aunty Zoe," he said.

"I was talking hypothetically," Zoe told her nephews. "You know, just using it as an example."

Caleb waved his fork at her excitedly.

"I don't care if you was being pathetic. When are we going to Disneyland?"

It took a full five minutes for the children to understand that a trip to Disneyland was not in the foreseeable future. Liam laughed to himself throughout and Zoe threw him more than one irritated glance.

He looked so damned at home amongst her brother's family. She could see no hint of unease between him and Tom, despite their years of estrangement. Yet she felt on tenterhooks, her nerves on edge.

Her unease ratcheted up another notch when Tom and Liam fell to reminiscing after their meal. She listened to stories from school and memories from their shared domestic life for as long as she could stand it before excusing herself to play with the children.

For a full twenty minutes she immersed herself in the game of tag her nephews had invented, teaming up with Rachel to ensure the little girl had a fair chance. Periodically she glanced to where Liam lounged with Tom and Jane, the three of them talking and laughing. Every time Liam's low, deep laugh sounded, something in her chest tightened.

She resented the way he made her feel. Weak, helpless, out of control. Fifteen again, basically. Totally at the mercy of her hormones and emotions.

But she wasn't a girl anymore; she was a woman. And she was in control of herself. Absolutely she was.

Which was why she was hiding in the yard, playing tag with the children.

The moment she acknowledged what she was doing, she left

the children to their game and crossed to the patio. She refused to let Liam send her into a spin. This was her family, her brother. If anyone should be feeling the outsider, it should be Liam.

He was pushing back his chair as she approached. "Great catching up again, Tom. Thanks for all your help," Liam said as he stood.

A wash of relief hit her—he was going. Thank God. Maybe now she could enjoy her visit with her nephews and niece minus complications or aggravations.

Tom's gaze slid to Zoe then back to Liam again as the two men shook hands.

"It was good to see you. Don't be a stranger," Tom said.

Zoe frowned as Liam turned to thank Jane for her hospitality. There had been something in her brother's eyes just now. He'd looked…uneasy. Almost guilty. She studied Tom's face but he kept his attention fixed on Liam. She shrugged and decided she must have imagined the small moment.

The kids insisted on giving Liam a big send-off, complete with waves from the front porch. Zoe hung back beside Jane as Tom walked Liam out to where his black SUV was parked in the street. The two men stood talking quietly for a few minutes more. She couldn't hear what they were saying, but her brother gestured toward Liam's car, then turned to look at Zoe briefly. Again she saw a flash of guilt on his face. He said something but Liam shook his head and talked intently for a few minutes. Finally they shook hands and Liam got in his car and drove off.

"What's going on?" Zoe asked when Tom rejoined her and Jane.

"What? Nothing," Tom said.

Zoe narrowed her eyes. Before she could probe further, Jane looped her arm through Zoe's.

"Why don't you stay for dinner, as well?" Jane said. "The

kids have been working through their favorite movies again lately. I think *Finding Nemo* is tonight's offering."

Zoe thought about an evening on the couch with her brother's children. Jane would pop corn, and her brother would con his wife into giving him a foot massage. If Zoe was lucky, she'd wind up with Rachel asleep in her arms like the last time they'd watched a movie together.

"Sure. That sounds nice," she said.

"Good stuff. Meanwhile, we can have another coffee and you can tell me about this bike of Liam's you're going to paint," Tom said.

"Just don't go getting any ideas," Jane admonished as she headed to the kitchen to put the kettle on. "There's no way I'm wallowing around corners in the family wagon while you cruise around on a custom motorbike."

"I'm not stupid. I know you're far too insecure about how hot I'd look riding a big custom chopper to let me buy one," Tom said, deadpan.

Zoe left them to their sparring and headed for the bathroom. She'd washed her hands and was on her way to the kitchen when she glanced into the study and stopped in her tracks.

When she'd painted the pieces for Tom's office, she'd gotten a little carried away and come up with too many canvases. Tom had hung the superfluous three paintings in his home study, assuring her he was thrilled to have enough to go round.

But the walls of his study were blank today, utterly bare. Her paintings were gone.

She was surprised at the stab of hurt she felt. Obviously her brother had not liked them as much as he'd assured her he did. How long had he left them on the walls before he took them down? A month? A week?

She returned to the kitchen feeling more than a little

subdued. Jane shot her a searching look and Zoe forced a smile. Jane sighed.

"You saw the study, didn't you?" she asked.

"It's fine. I understand. They were very bright, and probably really overwhelming in a small room," Zoe said quickly.

Tom looked up from where he was spooning coffee into a French press. He and Jane exchange a loaded glance. Tom put the packet of coffee down.

"Okay. Good. I wasn't very comfortable not telling you, but I knew you'd kick up a stink if we did and I wanted you to have the opportunity," he said.

Zoe stared at her brother.

"Could you repeat that in English?" she asked.

"Liam wanted to show your work to a friend of his who has an art gallery. I gave him the paintings from my office and the ones from the study here at home. That's why he was here today, to collect your art," Tom said.

Zoe blinked a few times, unable to quite believe what she was hearing.

"Liam is showing my stuff to his friend. And you were keeping it a secret from me?" she asked, her voice high with outrage.

Jane stepped forward and slid an arm around Zoe's shoulders. "I knew you'd be angry, but I was overruled."

"Arrogant, overbearing, pigheaded son of a bitch," Zoe said.

She was already turning on her heel, heading for the door before the last words were out of her mouth.

"I think that was for Liam, not you," she heard Jane explaining to her brother.

"Hell, yes, it is," Zoe said over her shoulder. "Where does he get off, trying to rearrange my life behind my back? I'm not a kid anymore. When is he going to get that through his thick skull?"

The front door slammed behind her as she strode toward her car.

Unbelievable. Liam Masters had apparently mistaken her for the kind of woman who liked having her life ordered for her. He was about to get a rude awakening—in the shape of her size-eight biker boot up his butt.

Deep inside, humiliation burned. She'd bared her soul to him yesterday and the first thing he'd done was take steps to give poor little Zoe a helping hand.

She didn't need anything from him. She didn't need anything from anyone. The sooner he got that straight, the better.

LIAM GOT THE CALL from Tom when he was ten minutes from his house. He figured he had a twenty-minute start on Zoe, so when he got home he went ahead with his original plan and carried the seven canvases into his dining room. He'd already decided that the bare floor and white walls were the perfect foil for Zoe's work, the next best thing to his own gallery. He worked quickly and steadily to position seven picture hooks around the room. He was sliding the last canvas into place when he heard the screech of tires in his driveway.

Only Zoe could keep up a head of steam through a half-hour drive. Right on cue she thumped on his front door.

"I want my paintings back," she said when he opened the door. She pushed past him into the house. "And I quit. I don't want anything to do with you and your bloody over-bearing do-gooderism. I am not your freaking charity project, Liam Masters."

She stood with her hands on her hips, shoulders proud.

"Zoe," he said.

She made a low, growling noise.

"Don't even bother. I don't give a shit what patronizing,

reasonable, generous explanation you have all worked out. This is my life you're rearranging to suit yourself. It's my life and my art. Who the hell do you think you are, sneaking behind my back to show it to some gallery owner?"

"Would you have let me if I told you what I wanted to do?"

"No. No way. I don't need your charity," she said.

"It's not charity to help out a friend."

"A friend," she said scathingly. "Is that what we are now? *Friends?*"

"It's what I'm trying to be, although you make it pretty damn hard."

Zoe was suddenly in his face, her fists thumping into his chest, the weight of her attack sending him staggering back a step.

"I don't want you to try to do or be anything for me. Just leave me alone."

He grabbed her fists. She was strong, despite her slim build, and he had to exert himself to hold her still.

"Calm down," he said.

She twisted her arms, trying to escape. He hauled her so close they were breathing into each other's faces. He could see the anger in her eyes, but he could also see the pride and, beneath that, the fear.

Suddenly he understood.

"It's not because I feel sorry for you, Zoe," he said quietly.

She froze, then she gave one last, hard yank on her wrists and he let her go. She stepped away from him and crossed her arms over her chest.

"Why, then? Why are you so gosh-darned fired up to help poor old Zoe?"

"I like you."

She stared at him. "That's it?"

"Yeah. Do I need a better reason? I've got a million, but

none of them are as good. I owe your parents. I hurt you in the past. I think you're bloody talented."

Zoe stared at him. Her hands were shaking when she raised them to push her hair away from her face.

"Damn you, Liam."

She turned her back on him and walked into his living room. He followed, stopping within arm's reach.

"Why do you always make it so hard?" she asked, her back still to him.

"What's so hard about me liking you?"

She looked at him over her shoulder.

"Because it's dangerous. And you know it. It takes us both to a place we don't want to go."

He didn't know what to say to that, because it was true.

Silence stretched between them. Zoe broke it by taking a deep breath and letting it out slowly. Then she scrubbed her face with her hands and turned to face him.

"Where are my paintings?" she asked.

For a moment he hesitated, weighing the merits of trying once again to talk her around. She held his eye, her gaze steely. He shrugged and led her to the dining room without saying another word.

Her eyes widened as she saw how he had hung her work, how the empty room and white walls allowed her art to speak for itself.

"They look good, don't they?" he said. "Kind of like they would if they were hanging in a gallery."

She shot him an unreadable look. Slowly she did a circuit of the room, her whole body radiating tension.

"Who is this gallery person, anyway?" she finally asked.

He knew exactly how much it had cost her to ask the question.

"Her name's Jacinta Hartman. She has a gallery in Toorak."

Zoe rolled her eyes. "Are you kidding? There's no way some rich bitch from Toorak is going to be interested in my stuff."

"I think she will be. I think you have no idea how good your *stuff* is."

"And you're an art expert now, are you?"

"I've seen enough over the years to know that people will eat up your work up with a spoon," he said.

Zoe made a rude noise.

"Don't believe me? Jacinta will be here in an hour," he said. "Hang around and hear what she says for yourself."

Zoe shifted her weight. He could see her brain ticking over, could feel her uncertainty warring with her desire to believe.

"What have you got to lose?" he asked.

She glared at him. "God, I don't know. Pride? Confidence? Nothing important."

"So if she doesn't like your work you'll never pick up a paintbrush again, is that it?"

Her lip curled in instant rejection of the idea. He smiled.

"So, tell me again, what have you got to lose?" he asked.

She opened her mouth to say something but instead huffed out an exasperated breath.

"You are a pushy pain in the ass, you know that?" she said.

Crossing to her, he hooked an arm around her neck and kissed her once, very firmly, on the mouth.

"Smart decision. You want a beer while we wait?"

She used her elbow to push him away, but she followed him into the kitchen.

Neither of them said a word as he got two beers from the fridge and slid one of them across the counter toward her. She twisted the top off and took a pull. Then she put the beer down, wiped her hands down the front of her jeans, lifted the beer again and began picking at the label. She frowned intently, as though the small task required all her concentration.

He leaned against the counter and watched her, touched and annoyed by her stubborn self-containment. Zoe would rather chew glass than admit she was nervous, now that she'd agreed to let a stranger assess her art. She hated letting anyone know she cared about anything.

"What's she like, this Jacinta woman?" Zoe asked after a few minutes.

"Smart. Savvy. She's been dealing art for nearly fifteen years. The gallery is a family business."

"How do you know her?" Her glance was penetrating, searching.

"We're friends. I met her at a client's Christmas party a few years ago."

She returned to picking at the beer label. He decided to take pity on her.

"Want to watch some TV while we wait? Or there's a pool table out back?"

"Pool sounds good."

They played two games in near silence. He breathed a sigh of relief when the doorbell rang. She was so tense, she was making him nervous. He headed for the door, but Zoe hung back. He called to her as he crossed the living room.

"Don't be shy. You'll like Jacinta," he said.

"I'm not shy," Zoe said.

It was enough to draw her after him and she was standing behind him when he opened the door.

"I'm early. Hope you don't mind," Jacinta said.

She stepped forward in a cloud of perfume and kissed his cheek. As usual she was dressed sleekly and stylishly in black, her skirt pencil slim, her shoes high and elegant.

"Now, where's this art you're going to dazzle me with?" she asked.

Then she registered Zoe hovering in the background.

"This is Zoe Ford, the dazzler," Liam said. "Zoe, this is Jacinta Hartman."

Zoe gave him an angry look before shaking Jacinta's hand.

"Don't listen to him. He doesn't know what he's talking about," Zoe said.

She was about to start talking herself down, making excuses so that the rejection she anticipated wouldn't sting quite so much. It infuriated him that she had so little faith in herself. It also made him want to kick something. Once upon a time, Zoe had never been afraid of anything.

He leveled a finger at her.

"Shut up," he said. "Not another word, okay?"

Jacinta threw him a startled look. Zoe flushed red and opened her mouth to blast him.

He placed a hand in the small of Jacinta's back and urged her toward the dining room. He heard Zoe's breath hiss out, then the determined sound of her footsteps dogging him.

"That was a little uncalled-for, don't you think?" Jacinta asked him quietly as they stepped into the dining room.

"When you know Zoe a little better, you'll understand," he said.

Jacinta raised an eyebrow and turned her attention to the paintings.

"Could I have a word with you, Liam?" Zoe asked from the doorway.

She was furious—again. He ignored her. He was busy watching Jacinta's face, noting the way her eyes narrowed briefly before her expression became smooth and unreadable.

Her business face. Which mean she liked Zoe's art. She liked it a lot, if he was any judge of her mannerisms. His shoulders relaxed. His gamble hadn't been for nothing, then.

"What do you think?" he asked.

Jacinta leaned forward to study Zoe's largest painting more closely. Zoe remained in the doorway, radiating resentment and anger.

"You mostly work with an airbrush?" Jacinta asked, glancing at Zoe.

Zoe blinked, surprised at the direct question. Liam hid a smile as he watched her try to work out how to respond. Rudely, and jeopardize the opportunity? Politely, and risk losing all her righteous indignation? Or something in between the two extremes?

"Yes. I use brushes, too, sometimes. Mostly I work with acrylics," Zoe said.

"You got any more like these?" Jacinta asked.

Zoe stood a little straighter.

"Yes," she said. Then she hesitated. "Why?"

"I like your work," Jacinta said boldly. "I can think of half a dozen of my clients who would kill to have something like this in their homes or offices. Especially with the kind of pedigree they come with."

Zoe frowned. "Pedigree? I don't know what Liam's told you, but I don't have any formal training or anything like that."

Jacinta crossed to stand in front of Zoe, her gaze scanning the other woman from top to toe.

"You're young, sexy, beautiful and edgy. That tattoo on your neck alone is enough to give you cred. Trust me, people are going to want to buy a little piece of you, Zoe."

Zoe blinked. Again he could see uncertainty warring with hope inside her. She wanted so much to believe in this good news, but life had taught her to be undemanding in her expectations.

"I have some more canvases under my bed at my apartment," she said slowly.

Jacinta laughed. "Perfect. We'll put that in the advertising copy. Please tell me you're living in a grungy garret somewhere?"

"It's a studio apartment," Zoe said. She sounded a little dazed.

Jacinta clapped her hands together, delighted.

"This tattoo on your neck—are there more?"

Zoe turned and lifted her T-shirt to display her back.

"Fantastic! Definitely a backless dress for the opening. Something a bit feral and sexy from one of the young designers in Fitzroy or Northcote." Jacinta started fumbling in her handbag. "Damn. I left my organizer at the gallery."

She closed her eyes and tapped her forefinger on her pursed lips.

"I think I have a week open in August. That would give you time to work on some more pieces, yes?" Jacinta asked.

"I guess." Zoe was pale, and he noted that her hands were shaking again. Not from anger this time, he guessed.

Jacinta nodded decisively. "I need to confirm dates, but I'll get back to you. In fact, why don't we all do dinner tomorrow night? I'll introduce you to Frederick, my PR guy. We can come up with a bit of a strategy."

"Um, okay. Sure. That sounds good," Zoe said.

Jacinta turned to Liam.

"Well, I was sure you were wasting my time, but I'm glad I came. Who would have thought? Liam Masters has an eye for art."

"I know what I like," he said.

Jacinta bounced a look between him and Zoe. "So I see. Well, there go the rest of my plans for the evening. *C'est la vie.*"

She crossed to Zoe's side and leaned in to kiss her.

"I'll see you tomorrow night," she said.

Liam escorted her to the front door, very aware of Zoe's gaze on his back as he left the room.

"Thank you, thank you, thank you," Jacinta said when they reached the front door. He'd never seen her so animated. "Do you have any idea how much money your friend is going to make me?"

"I'm more interested in what you can do for her, actually," he said dryly.

"Of course you are. I saw that the moment I walked in the door."

Jacinta cocked her head and studied him.

"I always wondered what it would take to really rev your engine. Now I know."

He frowned. "Zoe and I are friends. Period."

Jacinta patted his cheek. "Whatever."

Liam tensed. Was it that obvious that he wanted Zoe? Had Tom and Jane picked up on the same vibes at their house this afternoon? Was that why Zoe had said that him liking her was dangerous?

"It's not what you think," he said.

"Maybe it's not what *you* think. Ever thought of that?" Jacinta said.

She gave him a killer smile and exited. Liam shut the door and walked slowly to the dining room. It was empty. He frowned, then checked the kitchen, the living room and finally the games room.

Zoe was leaning against the edge of the pool table, rolling a billiard ball back and forth between her hands. She glanced at him when he came in. They stared at each other in silence for a long beat.

"I'm sorry for being such a pain in the butt," she said finally. She was frowning. He bet she hadn't had a lot of practice apologizing.

"Consider it forgotten."

"Thank you for getting your friend to look at my stuff."

He wondered how long it would be before Zoe referred to her work as art. A while, he suspected.

"I rang a friend. It's no big deal."

She shook her head. "It is, and we both know it."

Tension crackled in the air as they stared at each other again.

"I think I'd better go," she said.

He didn't try to stop her as she left the room. He'd done what he wanted to do—given her a head start. The small break she needed to get where she deserved to be. The rest was up to her and Jacinta and fate. It was time for him to step back and let Zoe go.

He followed her as she strode through his house to the front door. Her hair swung against her back, dark and silky. Her hips swayed from side to side. He breathed in her scent every step of the way.

She stopped on the threshold.

"I meant what I said. I'm sorry for being such a pain in the ass. Not that I like being treated like an idiot kid, but I understand how you might have felt I'd given you some justification to sneak around behind my back."

He slid his hands into his jeans pockets.

"I'll see you tomorrow," he said.

She nodded once and stepped out into the night. He forced himself to shut the door, all his reasons for keeping his distance circling in his head.

He had nothing to offer her. She'd wind up hurt. She deserved more.

Need beat a fierce counter-tattoo in his belly. He'd wanted her from the moment he set eyes on her in the Fords' kitchen all those years ago, and he'd never stopped wanting her. Might as well ask the tide to stop turning or the sun from rising. Zoe Ford was his own personal siren, the one woman who had always been able to burrow beneath his skin.

But he'd let her go tonight. And he'd keep letting her go. If it killed him.

He walked toward the living room. His steps slowed as he registered something: he hadn't heard Zoe's car start up.

He turned toward the front door. Two strides and he had it open. Sure enough, her car still sat in his driveway. He could see her behind the wheel, could see her hands on the steering wheel.

She hadn't gone home.

She didn't want to go.

He started toward the car.

9

WHAT ARE YOU DOING? she asked herself for the hundredth time as Liam circled the car to the driver's door. She'd left his house because she'd been dangerously close to giving in to the need to touch him again. She'd been sensible, so bloody sensible.

And now she'd ruined it by sitting out here in his driveway, waiting for him to do precisely what he was doing. Waiting for him to come for her.

"You idiot," she told herself as he reached for the handle.

Cool night air rushed in as the door opened. She stared at Liam. His face was hidden in shadow, his eyes unreadable.

What did she want to see there, anyway? Need? Desire? Some sign that he felt as compelled to be with her as she was to be with him?

I don't know what I want.

What a lie. She knew what she wanted. She was simply too smart, too cynical to imagine it was hers for the taking.

Liam sank into a crouch so that his eyes were on a level with hers. The weak glow of the interior light washed across his face.

"Something wrong?" he asked.

Yes. I don't want to go home. I want to touch you and taste you. I want to imagine for just a little while longer that this might happen between us.

"No."

Liam reached out and slid her keys from the ignition. He stood, the keys dangling from one finger.

"Hey," she said, much too late.

"You want 'em? Come and get 'em," he said. Then he walked toward the house.

She took a deep breath. She got out of the car. She followed him into the house. He was just disappearing around the turn in the staircase when she entered the living room.

She followed, her heart thumping loudly in her ears. Her thoughts kept time with her heartbeat: *What am I doing? What am I doing? What am I doing?*

He was pulling his T-shirt over his head when she pushed open his bedroom door. The smooth muscles of his chest and arms flexed as he tossed the T-shirt into a corner. She felt a little dizzy as his hands slid to the waistband of his jeans. His erection jutted large and proud as he pulled his jeans down.

She reached for the hem of her tank top and pulled it over her head. Seconds later she kicked her own jeans to one side. Her panties were next, then her bra. Liam watched her, his gaze smoky. She walked across the space that separated them and didn't stop until she was pressed against his body, her breasts flattened against his hard chest, his cock pressing into her belly.

She opened her mouth to tell him what a big mistake this was, but he kissed her. His hands smoothed down the sides of her body and onto her backside. She murmured restlessly as his fingers slid low over her cheeks, dipping between her thighs to where she was wet for him.

"I can't get you out of my head," Liam said as he began to kiss his way across the arch of her eyebrow. "I want you all the time, Zoe."

She shivered as a single finger slid inside her. Her muscles clenched around his invasion, wanting so much more.

"I'm sorry about yesterday. I shouldn't have pushed. And I shouldn't have gotten angry," he said.

She didn't want to talk about yesterday. She didn't want to think or talk at all. She pushed him backward until he was on his back on the bed. Then she straddled him and reached for his cock. Only the fullness of him inside her would satisfy the ache she felt. She slid onto him with one smooth tilt of her hips. He let his breath out in a rush. She began to ride, lifting her hips to the point where he almost slipped free before driving herself down on him, taking him as deep as he could go.

One of his hands began to tease her breasts, plucking her nipples, rolling them, squeezing them. His other hand slid between their bodies to the hot, wet place where they were joined. She let out a moan of encouragement as his thumb found her clit, gliding over and over it as his cock stroked her from the inside.

"Come for me, baby," he said, his voice very low and deep. "Come for me, Zoe."

Her back arched. Desire tightened inside her. She closed her eyes as the tension inside her became almost unbearable.

Then she was awash with pleasure, her body rippling with it, milking him, her muscles tightening around him. She felt him thrust up into her once, twice, three more times, then she felt the hot rush as he came.

He wrapped his arms around her and drew her down to lie across his chest. He was still inside her, still a part of her. A warmth that had nothing to do with sex and everything to do with the way he caressed the nape of her neck and cradled her so gently crept through her.

Her cynical self curled its lip.

You're riding for a fall, it shouted in the back of her mind.

She knew she should listen. She'd been hurt so many times before. But this was Liam. He'd always been her weak spot.

They made love twice more before she gathered her clothes and dressed in the dark. She'd waited until Liam's breathing was deep and steady before rolling from the bed, but she could feel him watching her as she tugged on her jeans.

Neither of them said a word as she collected her car keys from the bedside table. What was there to say, after all? They both knew that it had been a mistake.

They made the same mistake the next night, after dinner with Jacinta at the exclusive Vue du Monde restaurant in the heart of the city. Zoe felt acutely self-conscious in her one decent dress—black, discreet, conservative—and good-girl high heels. Jacinta and Frederick were studies in slick minimalism— perfect hair, perfect business suits, perfect everything. Only Liam looked like himself in a pair of dark denim jeans and a black silk knit T-shirt. His only concession to the venue was a jacket in fine charcoal suede. Somehow, without asking, Zoe knew that Jacinta had bought it for him. Which meant that they were lovers—or had been, at some time in the past.

She told herself she didn't care, that what he did when he wasn't with her wasn't her business, just as what she did when he wasn't around wasn't his. But the moment they were alone in his car on the way back to her apartment, she'd been unable to stop herself from asking what Jacinta meant to him and if the other woman knew Liam was screwing Zoe at the same time that he was doing her.

Liam had pulled over on the side of the road without saying a word and hauled her into his lap. He didn't let her go again until she was sweaty and trembling from the hottest, fastest climax she'd ever had. He'd zipped himself up and driven her the rest of the way home, and once again neither of them had mentioned what had happened between them. She wasn't sure what he was thinking—ignore it and it will go away?

Make hay while the sun shines?—but she'd long ago faced the fact that she had no control where he was concerned.

It didn't matter what she told herself. It was no longer enough to remember his words—*I'm not good relationship material*—or the lessons life had taught her regarding men and her unsuitability for a long-term relationship. She craved Liam. At work, she listened for the sound of his voice. When she wasn't with him, her fingers itched to pick up the phone. Every moment her mind wasn't busy with the mechanics of whatever she happened to be doing she defaulted to thinking about him.

The breadth of his shoulders.

The depth of his voice.

His long, strong fingers.

Might as well admit to herself that she was lost, an absolute goner. As besotted and obsessed with him as she'd ever been when she was a kid.

She'd fallen in love with Liam Masters. Again. Despite all her determination not to. Despite her fear and her certainty that it would only lead to heartbreak.

She faced the ugly, terrifying truth as she watched Liam's rear car lights fade into the darkness after he'd dropped her at her apartment post dinner and roadside sex.

She'd wanted him to stay. Wanted to invite him upstairs to her apartment and into her bed and her arms and her body. Wanted more of what he'd just given her in the car.

Who was she kidding? She wanted everything.

Nausea churned in her belly as she stripped her dress and stockings and underwear and stepped into the shower.

She wanted to cook for him in his too-big bachelor kitchen. She wanted to be the one to help him choose furniture for his dining room and his living room and all the other empty or underfurnished rooms in his house. She wanted to paint canvases for him to fill his house with color and life and energy.

She wanted the right to walk into his office at Masters Mechanics and slide her arms around him and lift her face for his kiss, out in the open, for everyone to see.

She wanted to be his. And she wanted him to be hers.

She laughed into the shower spray, but it wasn't funny. It was sad. And it was scary.

As she toweled herself dry and got into bed, she acknowledged that she wasn't going to walk away from him. She'd tried to resist him and it hadn't worked. She'd tried to contain their relationship to the merely physical, but that hadn't flown, either.

Staring at the ceiling, her fingers once again tracing her scar over and over, Zoe understood that she was weak enough and needy enough and hopeful, God help her, enough to take whatever she could get of Liam's life, mind and body. He liked her. He'd said it to her face, hadn't he? He obviously cared for her—he'd given her a job, hooked her up with Jacinta. And he still seemed to desire her, if tonight's display in the car was anything to go by.

It was enough. It would have to be. She would hang on to it and ride this thing out until the messy end. Then she'd get up and dust herself off again, as she had so many times before.

A single tear squeezed out from beneath her tightly closed eyelids. She felt it slide across her cheek and onto her pillow.

She'd tried to be smart, she really had. Somehow she'd wound up being really stupid.

ZOE WAS GOING TO BE ALL RIGHT. If he'd had any doubts about it, dinner with Jacinta and Frederick had well and truly put them to bed. Jacinta had confirmed that Zoe would have a show at her gallery in the first week of August. The pricing she was suggesting for Zoe's works had made Zoe gasp. If even half her paintings sold, she wouldn't have to work for a year. And if her work sold that well, the odds were good

Jacinta would keep her busy with commissions and other shows. Zoe was set. A new career, a new direction. New faith in herself. A dream to pursue.

There was no earthly reason for him to keep playing guardian angel in her life. His mission to help her to happiness was over. It was time for him to take a step back. Stop sleeping with her. Stop thinking about her. Every day he woke with new resolve to stand his ground and let her slip away. And every night he found some excuse to get his hands on her.

Monday night it was in the car on the way home from dinner with Jacinta and Frederick. Tuesday night they both worked late at the workshop and he ordered pizza for dinner. By the time it arrived, he'd had Zoe on his desk, her cries echoing around the empty workshop.

Wednesday night her car wouldn't start and he drove her home. She'd hesitated as she exited the car, then looked back over her shoulder and asked if he was coming inside.

Thursday night he got all the way home before he realized he was kidding himself. He called her up and asked her to meet him at his favorite Italian restaurant in Lygon Street, Carlton. They ate spaghetti Bolognese and crunchy garlic bread with the house wine. Afterward, he took her on a tour of the city on the back of his chopper, concluding with a circuit of the long, snaking roads that wound through Studley Park in the city's inner east end. Parked at one of the lookouts that provided spectacular views of the city skyline, he'd kissed and touched her till they were both more than a little bit crazy. Then he'd taken her back to his house and made love to her for hours.

Tonight, Friday, he stood in his office doorway watching her pack up her airbrush and paint supplies. He told himself that tonight would be the first night that he'd let her go home alone.

You weak bastard, a voice said in the back of his mind. *At least be honest with yourself if not Zoe.*

Because there was no way he was letting her go.

Maybe if she hadn't been wearing jeans that hugged every smooth curve of her hips and butt he'd have half a chance. Maybe if she didn't have her hair piled high on the back of her head, exposing the provocative tattoo around her neck, and maybe if he hadn't been haunted by her scent all day.

Zoe Ford had been the girl of his dreams, and now she was the woman who stood center stage in his life. He couldn't imagine a time when he wouldn't want her. He couldn't imagine a time when he wouldn't place her happiness above his own.

As he stood watching her, when he really wanted to be holding her, he forced himself to acknowledge the truth— she'd stayed with him through the years, buried deep inside him. And now he'd found her again and he wasn't sure he had the strength to let her go a second time.

And sometimes, like right now as he watched her push a strand of hair out of her eyes, he wondered why he had to give her up at all.

She could move in with him. She could continue to explore her art both at the workshop and via Jacinta and the gallery. They could argue and make love and make each other laugh and grow old together.

He pushed the thought away. He couldn't allow himself to start contemplating the life he could have with Zoe if he invited her home tonight and didn't let her go again.

Liam pushed himself away from the door frame and forced himself to return to his desk.

He wasn't the man for Zoe. He had scars all over his body and an almost constant ringing in his ear from his long-ago perforated eardrum to remind him of exactly why.

"Okay, that's me. I'm off."

He looked up to find her standing in the doorway.

"I guess I'll see you Monday, then," he made himself say.

She nodded. He could see she was disappointed he hadn't mentioned the weekend, or even asked what she was doing tonight.

You need to end it, he told himself.

"Your neighbor still looking in on Lucky and the kittens for you?" he asked instead.

"Yes."

"Want to have dinner?" he asked.

Both of them ignored the fact that five seconds ago he'd just indicated he wouldn't see her till Monday. They'd been playing this game all week, back and forth, neither of them acknowledging what they were circling around.

"What were you thinking?"

"Fish and chips on the beach?"

She nodded. "Sounds good."

He closed his eyes as she exited his office. He really was a weak prick. He knew what he had to do and it wasn't going to get any easier.

So much for putting Zoe's happiness first. But why should he be surprised? His father had been a selfish, possessive asshole, too.

The thought sent a chill down his spine. He almost called Zoe back. But he didn't. Because he was weak.

She was waiting in front of his house when he pulled into the driveway. He heard her footsteps on the pavement as he exited the Mustang. Then she was standing in front of him, a smile on her face. Somehow she managed to look cocky and vulnerable at the same time. Sexy and uncertain. Brave and scared.

He pulled her close, combing his fingers into her hair as he kissed her. She opened to him easily. He was hard in seconds as she pressed herself against him. She trailed kisses down his neck to his chest, pulling the neck of his T-shirt out of the way so she could tongue his collarbone. Then she slid her hand beneath the waistband of his jeans to find his cock.

"Shut the garage door," she murmured against his chest.

He saw the wicked glint in her eyes. He hit the automatic door button as Zoe sank to her knees.

Man, she was unbelievable. He felt his cock spring free as she unzipped his jeans, then her hot, wet mouth was closing over him. He hissed in a breath as her tongue traced the head of his cock. She curled one hand around the back of his thigh to hold him close and took all of him at once.

He stood it for as long as he could then he pulled her up and away from him.

"Enough," he said when she started to protest.

He hustled her into the house. They made it to the living room before he had her on the couch, tugging her jeans off. She wrapped her legs around his hips as he slid inside her.

"Hard and fast," she begged. "Please."

He gave her what she wanted, loving the way her eyes went distant and smoky and the way she bit her lip and arched her back as her climax approached.

His own climax hit him and he stroked into her one last time, feeling her beginning to come apart around him. She cried out, her thighs clenching around his hips. He pressed his face into the soft skin beneath her ear and inhaled the smell of her. Spice and sex and Zoe. He could never get enough of it.

He rolled to one side afterward. Zoe levered herself up so that she was resting on an elbow. She stared at herself—naked from the waist down, still wearing her bra and long-sleeved T-shirt, her jeans discarded in a tangle a few steps away. She laughed, the sound low and earthy.

"You'd think we'd be able to at least get our clothes off by now," she said.

"Practice makes perfect," he said.

He wrapped an arm around her and pulled her close. He could feel her breath against his neck, warm and moist. He didn't want to let her go.

"So, those fish and chips you lured me over here with," Zoe said after a few minutes. "Were they real or just bait to get me to put out?"

"You want dinner *and* sex?" he asked, reluctantly letting her roll away from him.

She stood. "I'm high maintenance, baby. Haven't you worked that out yet?" She laughed.

He lifted his hips so he could drag his jeans and boxer-briefs back up. Zoe hopped on one leg as she pulled her underwear on. He eyed the shadows between her thighs and wanted to tear her underwear off all over again.

"Stop looking at me like that or we'll starve to death," she said.

The rumble of his stomach decided the issue. They tidied themselves and walked around the corner to the local shops. They ordered up big, and Zoe insisted on buying Coke to cut through the grease of their heart-stopping meal. Ten minutes later, a warm paper-wrapped bundle under his arm, he led her to the beach.

It was only dusk but the streetlights were already on along the shore. The sand was still warm from the sun and they found a spot near the seawall. He unwrapped their meal and watched Zoe attack the food with zeal.

Fifteen minutes later she collapsed back on the sand holding her belly.

"My God, I haven't had so much salt and grease in one hit in a long time. How can I feel so satisfied yet so guilty all at the same time?"

"I remember your folks used to order fish and chips every Friday night," he said, staring out at the ink-dark ocean. "I thought I was in paradise when I first came to live with you guys."

"Really? Don't tell me your mom was a health freak?"

He shrugged.

"To be honest, I can't really remember what she used to feed me. I know we didn't do takeout a lot. Couldn't afford it."

Zoe was silent for a moment.

"It must have been hard, watching her die. I can't even imagine how hard," she said finally.

He shrugged. "It was harder watching my dad lay into her. At least with the cancer I knew there was nothing I could do to stop it."

Zoe screwed the leftovers of their meal into a big paper ball and pushed it to one side. He felt the warmth of her body as she shifted closer to him, copying his knees-drawn-to-chest posture.

"There's no way you could have stopped your father, Liam. You were just a kid."

"Yeah."

She nudged him with an elbow.

"Is that a 'yeah, I know,' or a 'yeah, I still should have done something'?" she asked.

He shifted restlessly.

"He was a big guy. I tried to stop him a few times but it only made him angrier."

Why had he even mentioned his father? He hated talking about this shit.

"Have you ever heard from him?"

He stiffened. "No."

He could feel her looking at him.

"You ever wonder where he is, whether he's still alive…?"

Liam turned to meet her eyes. "No."

She nodded. "Fair enough."

Silence stretched between them for a few minutes as they both stared out at sea.

"I think about Marty Johannsen sometimes," she said after a while. "Whether he's married with kids, that kind of thing." She paused, then huffed out a breath. "Stupid, huh? It wasn't as though he tried to get me pregnant. But still… It didn't change his life, what happened that night. He can still have kids, a family."

A cool breeze blew off the water and she shivered. Liam dropped an arm around her shoulder and pulled her closer against his side.

"He never spoke to me afterward, you know. He and his mates used to laugh when I walked past them at school, but not once did he look me in the eye. And after my operation… Well, a lot of kids didn't look me in the eye after that. Like I was the school freak or something."

He knew how hard it was for Zoe to talk about the past and her feelings. He'd seen how much it had hurt her when he pushed her for the truth. He also knew that she was offering up her stories to make it easier for him to tell his. She wanted to know about his dad. She wanted to share his pain the way he'd shared hers.

He couldn't do it. Everything in him balked at the thought of unpacking all the ugliness he'd stowed away.

The warm weight of Zoe's head fell onto his shoulder. He felt the tickle of her hair against his jaw and forced himself to unclench his teeth.

"He was a drunk," he said quietly. "I can't remember seeing him sober. He must have been, because he had a job some of the time. But I can't remember seeing him without a glass or a bottle in his hand."

She remained silent, the only sound the breaking of the waves and the hum of traffic on the road behind them.

"Me and Mom used to gauge his mood by the way he came home. If he slammed the front door, we knew we were in for it."

He shook his head, remembering.

"He was a scary bastard. The first time we ran away and he came after us, I thought he'd killed her, she was so quiet afterward."

Zoe stirred beside him, turning so that she could wrap her arms and legs around him. Only then did he realize he was shaking.

"You don't have to tell me any more if you don't want to," she said.

She was soft and warm against him. He took a deep breath, then another. She leaned closer and pressed a kiss to his cheekbone.

"Let's go home," she said.

They dusted off the sand from their clothes and disposed of their leftovers. They were both cold after sitting for so long in the cool ocean breeze, and Zoe went straight to his en suite when they got home and started running a bath.

"I've always wanted to try this monster tub of yours out," she said as she started stripping her clothes.

They soaked for nearly an hour, washing each other's backs, talking about the comp bike, the business, her art, small incidents from the day. Afterward he toweled her dry and carried her to his bed where he made love to her for a second time.

Her sighs and caresses and the thump of her heart against his own made him want to draw it out for as long as he could. But finally he lost control and things got a little wild and crazy.

He woke to the increasingly familiar sound of Zoe dressing in the dark. He reached out to grab her when she stood up after zipping her boots.

"Don't go," he said.

"It's late," she said, gently trying to tug her arm free.

"Don't go," he repeated.

His words hung between them, heavy in the dark. He drew her toward him, pulled her onto the bed. He kissed her, ran his hands down her back.

"I want you to stay," he said against her lips.

Her breath eased out and her body relaxed.

"Okay."

She was staying. Something in his chest expanded at the thought. He would wake in the morning and find her beside him.

God, he loved her.

He stilled as the thought registered.

Jesus, when had that happened?

But he knew: it had happened the moment he looked into her eyes again after twelve long years.

Zoe wriggled in his arms, and he realized his hands were fisted in her clothing.

"You going to let me get undressed again?" she asked, amused.

He forced himself to release his grip. She moved away from him and he listened to the sounds of her clothes hitting the floor. Then the mattress dipped with her weight and she was sliding into bed next to him.

Emotion burned in his belly, expanded in his chest. He wrapped his arms around her and pressed his face into the warm skin of her neck. Zoe. His, at last. He felt as though he'd been waiting for this moment all his life.

No wonder he hadn't been able to walk away from her.

For a few short seconds, panic gripped him as he thought of his father and his mother and the promise he'd made to himself. Then Zoe's arms came around him and she rested her head on his chest.

Slowly his body relaxed as he gave himself up to it. It wasn't like he had a choice. He loved her. He always had.

10

FOUR WEEKS LATER Zoe stood with her eyes tightly closed, Liam's chest warm and solid behind her. His hands covered her eyes and his voice rumbled through her body every time he spoke.

"No peeking," he said.

"Stop fussing. I want to be surprised," she said.

She could hear the guys talking amongst themselves and the scuff of footsteps on the floor, along with the faint click of metal on metal. Nerves thrummed in her belly, sending adrenaline tingling into her fingertips.

This was it, the great unveiling of their competition chopper. She was about to see if her ideas had worked, if art and form and function had come together in a cohesive whole—or if between them they'd created Frankenstein's monster.

She wanted it to be good so much she felt a little sick. She wanted to make Liam proud, to repay his faith in her. She wanted the guys to be repaid for their welcoming camaraderie and easy friendship. And she wanted it to sing for her own sake, too, because she'd worked hard and wanted to be proud of what she'd achieved.

"Okay. Here we go," Liam said near her ear.

The warmth of his hands left her face and she opened her eyes. In front of her was a sleek, shiny motorcycle, its lines long, low and sexy. Her gaze traveled from the elongated front forks back to the handlebars, then along the body. Fat tires, chrome alloys and a custom-made, hand-tooled, cherry-red leather seat drew her eye next, but nothing commanded as much attention as the images that jumped out from the bike's fuel tank, fenders and oil pump. Zoe's avenging angel strained forward, power and determination in every line of her beautiful face and body. Purple and orange and red flames licked at the tips of her wings and her streaming hair, propelling her forward. More flames licked along the fenders and curled around the oil pump cover.

Zoe blinked and took a step backward. The bike looked incredible. She couldn't quite believe that she'd had a hand in creating it.

"Well, what do you think?" Liam asked.

She shook her head. "I don't know what to say. You guys have done an amazing job. The way you've shaped the exhaust pipe to echo the curve of her wings. And the gear shift… I honestly don't know what to say," she said. She reached out to caress the custom, chrome "suicide" gearshift, the head of which was a rounded, stylized heart in keeping with her old-school tattoo theme.

"Listen to Miss Modesty. This bike is made by your paint job, lady," Vinnie said. "If we don't win the build-off with this little puppy, I'll eat my boot."

The other guys added their agreement to Vinnie's, and Zoe flushed hotly, touched by their praise.

Liam's hands landed on her shoulders from behind and he leaned close.

"Suck it up, babe. I know it kills you to hear nice things about your work, but you'd better get used to it. Come August, you're going to have praise coming out the yoo-hoo once Jacinta has finished with you," he said.

She pushed an elbow back into his belly but he dodged

away, laughing. She turned to tackle him, but he grabbed her around the waist and before she knew it she was being lifted over her shoulder in a firefighter's carry. Liam spun in a circle, whooping and hollering, the guys yelling their encouragement. Zoe laughed with them, then slid a hand down the back of Liam's jeans to grab a handful of his boxer-briefs.

"Unless you want to sing like a soprano, you'd better put me down, caveman," she threatened.

The guys doubled up with laughter as Liam set her on her feet. Vinnie handed around beers and they all raised their drinks.

"To whipping butt at the build-off," Liam said.

"Bloody oath!" Vinnie said.

"And the rest," Paul said.

Zoe laughed and drank to the toast. Everyone fell to talking, circling the bike and admiring what their joint efforts had created. Zoe hung back a little, surprised by the buzz of achievement she felt. Creating a tattoo for someone was fulfilling but it was essentially a one-person occupation and she'd never felt like this at the end of a job. Working in collaboration with Liam and his crew had been fun, challenging and infinitely rewarding. Like being part of a big, dysfunctional, potty-joke-obsessed family.

Seeing her hovering, Paul called her over to ask how she'd finessed the flames on the oil pump cover. She was squatting beside him, admiring the cutouts in the alloy wheels when Liam joined them. His thigh was hard against hers as he crouched beside them.

"Hope you've got enough spare time in your schedule to take on some more paint jobs," he said. "Once this thing becomes public property everyone is going to want a Zoe Ford bike."

"Stop it," she said. "You don't have to keep blowing smoke up my skirt."

"I'm not. Trust me, in a few weeks' time you're going to be run off your feet trying to keep both me and Jacinta happy," Liam said.

She could see the sincerity and pride in him at what they'd achieved. She could also see something else, and her heart squeezed tight in her chest, just as it had every time she'd caught him looking at her in the same intense, warm way over the past few weeks.

Liam cared for her. He cared for her a lot. It was in every look he gave her, every caress, every word he threw her way.

She had to quell the impulse to reach out and cup his face. As happened so often lately, words crowded the back of her throat. But she couldn't—wouldn't—say them. Once, a long time ago, she had boldly declared her love for him. Life had taught her to be more cautious since then. For now, it was enough to look at him and understand that somehow, by some miracle, this thing between them was real and it wasn't going anywhere.

It had taken a while for her to work that out, longer still to accept it. After their first week together she'd stopped giving herself a hard time about how she felt and what she wanted. The simple truth was that she was a goner where Liam was concerned and she could do nothing but ride this thing out to its inevitable conclusion. There was no point trying to hold back or protect herself—she'd tried both strategies and failed dismally. She'd take what she could get, store away the memories and endure the pain as best she could when it came.

Still, she couldn't forget the fact that they hadn't spent a night apart since he'd asked her to stay that first Friday. And that he was the one who had asked her to stay the night, not the other way round. Then there was the way he made love to her: with a single-minded intensity and depth of emotion that made her tremble inside. At work, he sought her out constantly, casually touching her arm, her shoulder, her back as though he couldn't be near her and not make contact.

Every day the reality of their relationship reinforced what she so desperately wanted to believe—he was as invested as she was.

Maybe he even loved her, the way she loved him. Maybe one day soon he'd even say it out loud. And then, maybe, she'd find the courage to say it in return.

Dizzying thoughts. For now she contented herself with leaning on his shoulder as she pushed herself to her feet, giving him a surreptitious squeeze before she let him go. The guys all knew she and Liam had something going on—they weren't blind, after all—but by mutual, unspoken agreement she and Liam tried to keep things professional during work hours.

"What time's the truck coming tomorrow to take the bike to the build-off?" Vinnie asked as he flipped the cap off his second beer.

Liam had organized a spit roast and catering for the grand unveiling. Consequently, the boys were settling in for a big night.

"First thing, but don't worry, I've got it covered," Liam said.

He was one of the few who wouldn't have a hangover tomorrow, Zoe knew. He never drank to excess. After their talk on the beach, she understood why control was so important to him.

For a moment she was overwhelmed with a rush of tenderness as she watched him laugh with one of his crew leaders, his big body relaxed and at ease as he took a pull from his beer. He was a good man, despite the roadblocks life had thrown in his way. He was one in a million.

And he's mine. I get to take him home and make love to him. I get to hold him in my arms all night. I get to wake up with him tomorrow morning. And hopefully the morning after that, and the one after that.

The thought still felt tentative, uncertain, as though she was trying it on for size. But she was prepared to believe. She wanted to. After years of not believing, of not daring to dream, she had started to want things for herself again. And she wanted Liam, more than anything in the world.

He glanced at her. Their eyes met and his mouth curled slowly at the corners. Then his gaze dipped below her face and he gave her a long, slow, lazy head-to-toe. She could practically feel him touching her, his gaze was so hot. When he once again met her eyes his smile curved into a full grin.

Cocky bastard. Cocky, wonderful, generous, sexy bastard.

Because she couldn't stay away, she made her way to his side. He smiled at her, then gently clinked the neck of his beer bottle against hers in a silent toast.

Mine, she told herself again as she stared into his eyes.

Happiness welled up inside her. She smiled.

A month ago she would never have imagined any of this. Right now, right this minute, however, anything seemed possible.

THE FOLLOWING NIGHT Liam rested his elbow against the bar at Thrashed and waited for Zoe to come onstage. Or, more accurately, Vixen. Zoe had kicked him out of her change room half an hour ago before she started her transformation into her stage persona. He'd seen enough of her costume to know tonight was going to be one hell of a torturous experience. High heels, sheer stockings, a PVC miniskirt. The crowd was going to go nuts, as they had last time he'd seen her perform. And he was going to want to storm the stage and make it clear to every horny asshole in the audience that she was his.

He wasn't looking forward to it. On the other hand, there was a wildness in Zoe when she was onstage that spoke to something equally wild in him. He hadn't forgotten what had happened last time he'd visited her in her dressing room after a performance. This time around, he would watch her taunt and tease the crowd with what they couldn't have and know that he alone would get to touch her. He wasn't proud of it, but he was enough of a Neanderthal to get off on the idea.

There was movement onstage and a ripple of excitement went through the crowd. The lights flashed once, then dropped to darkness. Liam smiled to himself as the audience fell silent: Zoe sure knew how to milk a moment for all its drama.

The lights came up at the same time that the music kicked in. A spotlight found Zoe at center stage, both hands gripping the microphone, one long leg twined around the mike stand as she sang the opening lines. Her face was geisha white, her eyes black and heavy with sixties-style kohl, her eyeliner sweeping out from the corners of her eyes to give her an exotic Cleopatra look. Her mouth was a juicy, wet plum, a perfect match for the plum tank top she wore. The top was cropped to just below her breasts and he was almost one hundred percent certain she wasn't wearing a bra beneath it. The PVC skirt sat low on her hips and high on her thighs, a ridiculous strip of plastic that barely covered her ass. Sheer black stockings and black garters completed her ensemble.

She looked wild, wanton, sexy as all hell. The crowd whistled and howled its appreciation.

He ground his teeth. This was going to be a lot harder than he'd thought.

It was one thing to tell himself she was performing, that none of the men howling for her would ever come close to touching her, but it didn't stop him from feeling fiercely possessive. She was his. He adored her, admired her, needed her. He didn't want to look into a sea of faces and know they were all imagining her naked, wet and willing.

But he understood that Vixen was a very real part of Zoe's personality. She'd used her alter ego to reclaim power when she'd felt worthless as a woman. He would never ask her to lock away that part of herself, no matter how much it killed him.

By small degrees, he forced himself to relax and enjoy the show. Zoe had a great voice and she knew how to work the stage. Her band members were tight and knew what they were doing. As live performances went, it was entertainment with a capital *E*.

If only he didn't have the fierce, compulsive urge to cover her with a blanket, all would be good.

By the time Zoe was banging out the last song of the night, he was on his second beer and feeling almost sorry for the poor saps in the audience. Zoe hadn't let up, shaking her ass at them, teasing them mercilessly with her hot body. A lot of very horny men would be staggering out of the club tonight, if Liam had any guess.

The crowd erupted into applause as Zoe wailed the last notes and took a bow. After a few shout-outs to the crowd, the band exited the stage. Liam settled back to wait. It was tempting to join her in her dressing room, but he didn't want a quickie against the wall. After over an hour of sexual torture, he planned to inflict a little of his own once he got Zoe alone.

One heel hooked on the boot rail behind him, Liam slid his hand into his pocket. His fingers found the irregular edges of the key he'd had cut during the week. His front door key. For Zoe.

He'd meant to give it to her before the unveiling and ask her to move in with him but something had held him back. He'd never lived with a woman before. It went against all his rules. But he'd given up pretending he had any control where Zoe was concerned. Even though it scared him on a visceral, bone-deep level, he wanted to share his life with her.

He straightened as the stage door opened and Zoe emerged, her hair subdued into a ponytail, her face bare of makeup, jeans and a T-shirt replacing her provocative stage gear. Lust thumped low in his belly. Call him old-fashioned, but he much preferred her without all the bullshit.

His fingers curled around the key as he watched her weave her way toward him. He'd give it to her now, before they joined the rest of the band for pizza. Nerves danced in his belly, but he knew she'd say yes. Hoped she would, anyway.

She was halfway to the bar when three guys stepped in front of her. Liam tensed, then reminded himself that Zoe could more than handle herself. She'd given a couple of over-eager fans the stiletto treatment tonight when they tried to join her on the stage. He knew she wouldn't appreciate him interfering. Still, his gaze narrowed as he watched a thickset blond guy lean close to talk to her.

The expression on Zoe's face was the first giveaway that something was very wrong. Her face went blank with shock and from across the room he could see the color drain from her cheeks. She shook her head and backed away from the three men, but the blond guy followed.

Liam was already pushing his way toward them when recognition flashed in Liam's brain. He knew that blunt nose and thick neck and mean mouth. It had been twelve years, but he recognized him.

He could hear Zoe's voice rising in distress as he drew closer. "I don't want to talk to you. I have nothing to say to you."

Marty Johannsen spread his hands wide even as he loomed over her.

"Don't be like that, Zoe, baby. I've come all this way to see you after I heard about your little act. I've been telling my boys how we knew each other back in the day," he said, his smile suggestive.

Liam was two strides away when Johannsen made the mistake of reaching for her, grabbing her upper arm as he tried to halt her retreat. Zoe jerked backward, attempting to break his grip. As if in slow motion, Liam saw Johannsen's arm tense as he pulled her toward himself, dragging Zoe off balance. Liam could see the fear in her eyes, and his mind flashed to a hundred other memories of a woman wide-eyed with terror and fear. Then he was on the other man, his fist smashing into bone as animal instinct took over.

This was the man who had taken away Zoe's future. This was the weak shit who had taken advantage of her vulnerability and taken what he wanted without thought of the consequences—consequences Zoe would live with for the rest of her life. This was the man who hadn't had the guts to meet Zoe's eyes the day after he'd taken her virginity but who could turn up twelve years later to assert his bragging rights and see if he could get lucky again.

White-hot rage took over as Liam threw another punch then another. Johannsen staggered backward, reeling from the unexpected attack. Blood spurted as Liam smashed his fist into the other man's nose. Johannsen tried to draw up his arms to protect himself, but Liam was faster, stronger. Then Johannsen was on the ground and Liam was on top of him, pounding him with blow after blow. Vaguely he heard screams, felt someone tugging at his shoulders, trying to haul him off the other man. Then a thick arm snaked around his neck and he was being hauled backward.

He choked, struggling for air. His right arm was bent up his back and used to force him to his knees. Then the arm around his throat was gone and he could breathe again.

Panting, sweat dripping from his face, he lifted his head and saw what he'd done, the pulp he'd made of Marty Johannsen's face. Then he saw Zoe, a hand pressed to her mouth, tears in her eyes as she met his gaze.

He dropped his head, hating what he'd recognized in her face: fear.

Zoe was afraid of him.

It was his worst nightmare.

He was his father's son, after all.

ZOE'S ASS WAS NUMB from sitting on the hard wooden bench at the police station. Her stomach was hollow and empty, her eyes sore from lack of sleep. She'd been waiting for nearly ten hours—overnight, in fact—for Liam to be released.

He'd been charged with assault. She'd called Tom because she didn't know what else to do, and Tom had roped in a lawyer friend to take care of things. Lincoln Scott had arrived two hours ago, disappearing into the realms beyond the front desk. She hadn't heard a word since.

She rubbed her tired eyes. It had all happened so quickly—Marty appearing out of nowhere, trying to grab her, then Liam rushing past her, fierce and unstoppable. She'd tried to pull him off the other man, but it had taken the brawny bouncer to break up the fight. The police had arrived within seconds, closely followed by an ambulance. Liam had gone to the police station, Marty to the hospital.

Tom had offered to drive into town and wait with her, but she'd assured him she was okay, that she just needed help finding a suitable lawyer. The truth was, she was a million miles from okay.

Seeing Marty Johannsen after all these years had shaken her to her very foundations. The way he'd looked at her, the sound of his voice. Memories she'd long buried had risen up inside her—those horrible, painful minutes on the ground, Marty on top of her, his alcohol breath in her face. The shame in the weeks that followed. Then the guilt and anger in the months and years after her operation.

When he'd appeared in front of her so suddenly she'd recoiled instinctively, but he'd been determined to show off his great conquest to his buddies. She'd seen the way they all looked at her, as though she was for sale and Marty owned the deed of title. She could guess what he'd told them. Only now, twelve years after the fact, was he willing to own his part in what had happened between them, and only because Zoe Ford had suddenly become a scalp worth claiming.

He was beneath contempt. She disliked him so much she couldn't summon even a shred of disquiet or sympathy over what Liam had done to him. He'd recover from a broken nose and a few facial lacerations and go about his life as he always had. She would always be barren.

It was Liam she was concerned about. Lincoln Scott had revealed that Liam had an old assault charge from when he was nineteen. While it had been a long time between incidents, the wrong judge could choose to make an example of him. The thought of him going to jail for her was unbearable.

She stretched her legs in front of her and dropped her head against the wall.

She would never forget the look on his face when he'd met her eyes after the fight. On his knees, his arm bent up behind his back, sweat and blood dripping from his face. He'd looked broken, shattered. Numb. She'd tried to talk to him but he'd turned away. Then the police had arrived and they'd been separated.

He'd been protecting her from harassment but also avenging her, making up for past wrongs—his own and Marty's. She knew he blamed himself for leaving all those years ago, for not being there. And, of course, he blamed Marty for taking what she'd so drunkenly offered.

The sound of voices beyond the counter alerted her to new activity and she straightened. The opaque security doors darkened with the silhouettes of two figures. Then the doors slid open and Lincoln Scott exited with Liam.

Zoe stood. Tears filled her eyes as she saw the bruises on Liam's face, the swelling on his lip. His expression was closed, withdrawn.

"Are you all right? Did they let you see a doctor?" she asked, reaching for his arm, needing to touch him to reassure herself that he was okay.

"I'm fine," he said. He barely looked at her, instead turning to Lincoln.

"Thanks for your help. I appreciate it," he said. He offered the lawyer his hand.

"Not a problem. We need to make an appointment to discuss your defense. I'll call you later in the week."

"No defense. I'll plead guilty."

Zoe frowned.

"With your injuries, we've got a strong case for assault against Johannsen, as well," Lincoln said. "The best-case scenario all around is if both of you choose not to press charges against each other."

"No charges, no defense," Liam said firmly.

"Liam, he hit you, too. Look at your face. Why should he get off scot-free just because you won?" Zoe demanded.

Again Liam barely looked at her.

"We'll talk later in the week," he said to the lawyer.

Zoe followed Liam outside. What was going on? Was he angry with her because of the fight? Did he think that she'd incited it in some way with her provocative performance? Was that why he was being so cold?

"What's going on?" she asked once Lincoln had left to find his car.

"Nothing. Listen, I'll get a cab to my place. You should go home, try to get some sleep."

Still no eye contact. Zoe wanted to grab him and force him to look at her and tell her what was going on. Instead, she shook her head.

"I'm driving you home," she said.

He looked as though he wanted to argue, but he didn't. Traffic was heavy with the morning rush and they made the entire half-hour trip from the North Melbourne police station to St. Kilda in heavy silence. By the time she was pulling into his driveway, Zoe's stomach was churning with anxiety.

She didn't understand what was wrong, but she knew something was. Badly.

She followed him into the house, past the funky hat stand she'd made him buy the previous weekend and the hall table she'd picked out for him the weekend before that.

He stopped in the living room and turned to face her.

"Thanks for contacting Lincoln for me," he said.

She couldn't stand the distance he was putting between them and she moved closer and reached for his hand.

"What if we clean up your face before we do anything else, okay?" she said.

He pulled his hand free from her grasp. She met his eyes, and what she saw there made her heart contract in her chest.

"What's going on, Liam?" she asked for the second time that morning.

"This can't happen anymore, Zoe," he said.

She frowned.

"What? What do you mean?"

"I mean it's over. I don't want to see you anymore."

She flinched. This was the last thing she'd expected. Anger, perhaps. Frustration, definitely, and concern about the police involvement. But not complete rejection.

Hurt unfolded inside her, fresh but familiar.

"Right," she said.

She couldn't think. She stared at a spot on the floor, trying to pull her thoughts together.

"Is it because of what happened?" she asked after a few beats. "Because you got into a fight over me?"

"Something like that." He headed for the stairs.

She stared at his back, shock slowly giving way to dawning anger.

After five weeks of every night and every day, that was all the explanation she got?

She raced up the stairs after him. She found him in the bathroom, tugging his T-shirt over his head. She gasped when she saw the bruises on his chest and belly.

"Liam, my God, you need to see a doctor," she said.

She moved toward him but he stepped away from her.

"You need to go," he said.

"I'm not going anywhere until you've seen a doctor and we've talked properly."

"There's nothing to say. I've made my decision," he said.

"What about me? Don't I get a say?" she asked.

"No."

She blinked at his arrogance, then she registered his tension, the way he wouldn't let her touch him, the way he was standing so defensively, almost as though he was afraid to let her near.

"This is bullshit, Liam. Tell me what's really going on."

He closed his eyes. He looked infinitely weary, as though he'd been fighting a battle for a long time and only just admitted defeat.

"It doesn't matter. This was always going to happen. I told you, I'm not good relationship material. We were never going to be more than sex."

She shook her head, standing her ground.

"We've been about more than sex since we were teenagers, and you know it."

He stared at her. "Zoe. I'm doing this for you," he said.

"So am I. Tell me the truth, Liam. Tell me why you're not good relationship material." She took a deep breath, forcing herself to go to the scariest place she could imagine. "Or is this about me? Is this about me not being able to have children?"

She'd rather know the truth. She was almost certain of that, although it was going to hurt like hell if he admitted that, like all the others, he couldn't get past her essential emptiness. Right from the start, he'd never seemed to care. He'd seemed to see so much more in her than the scar on her belly and what it represented.

"Jesus, Zoe, no. This is nothing to do with you. You're… There's nothing wrong with you," he said.

She studied him, trying to keep her own hurt at bay as she sought to understand what was happening. None of it made sense to her. She had no idea how to get through to him. She had only one card left to play.

"Liam, I love you," she said quietly.

He stilled, then he sighed heavily, his shoulders sagging. He crossed to the bath and sat on the rim, his hands braced on his knees, his head lowered. He took a deep breath, then another.

"Don't I at least deserve the truth?" she asked.

He swore and lifted his head to look at her. His eyes glistened with unshed tears. He looked hunted, a man on the edge.

She took a step forward, needing to comfort him. He held up a hand.

"Don't," he said.

She ignored him, brushing his hand aside and sliding her arms around him. His head came to rest against her breasts as she embraced him, holding him tight, her hands smoothing down his back.

She loved this man and she didn't know what was wrong but she wasn't about to give him up without a fight.

LIAM SLEPT THROUGH THE DAY and woke when it was dark. He hadn't eaten in over twenty-four hours and he forced himself to swallow a bowl of cereal even though he wasn't hungry.

He'd done it. He'd told Zoe the ugly truth and set her free. He should feel lighter or at least moderately relieved that now she was safe.

He felt like shit.

He'd hurt her. He'd let things get out of hand between them. And now he had to live with the eternal punishment of having had Zoe and lost her.

Because he didn't know where to put himself, he did laps of the house, walking from the dining room to the kitchen to the living room in a never-ending circuit. Eventually he went back to bed. Sleep at least gave him a few hours' peace from his thoughts.

Zoe had finished her work at Masters Mechanics with the completion of the competition chopper so at least he didn't have to face her the next day when he went into the workshop. It didn't stop him thinking about her constantly. He wanted to call her, check on how she was doing. But he was the last person she would want to hear from.

He loved her more than anything or anyone and he'd hurt her. The knowledge sat in his gut all day, gnawing away at him.

By midafternoon he could stand it no longer. He phoned Tom, calling himself ten different kinds of pathetic as he talked around the subject, finally asking if he'd spoken to Zoe recently.

There was a short pause before Tom spoke. "She came over here yesterday."

Liam nodded. That was good. She'd gone to family. She had someone looking out for her. He cleared his throat.

"Okay. Good. I just wanted to make sure she wasn't doing anything too crazy," he said.

"You could always call her yourself, you know," Tom suggested.

"No," Liam said.

"If you want to grab a beer or something, I'll be leaving the office at around seven tonight," Tom said.

Again Liam was forced to clear his throat. The Fords had always come through for him. That was the kind of people they were.

"Thanks, mate, but I'll be all right," he said.

Liam sat with his hand on the phone receiver for a long time after the call had ended, tempted to pick it up and dial Zoe and damn the consequences. He battled with himself, forcing himself to remember the fear in Zoe's eyes and the terrifying moment when his temper had slipped its leash. He flexed his hand, staring at the rawness of his knuckles.

Remember who you are, where you come from.

ON TUESDAY Liam sent Vinnie to Sydney to attend the biker build-off judging. Liam had planned to go personally, but he couldn't concentrate, and the last thing he felt like doing was schmoozing a bunch of potential customers. He was still at his desk late on Tuesday night when Vinnie rang through to deliver the news: Masters Mechanics had come runner-up to Perth-based Western Choppers. Vinnie was pissed off and more than a little drunk. Liam reminded him that their chopper would still feature in a number of magazines and that they'd get more than their fair share of inquiries from the comp. When he hung up, all he could think about was that the news would give him an excuse to call Zoe.

He didn't. He'd broken it off with her. The least he could do was have the guts to stick to his own decision.

Later as he was at home picking at dinner in front of the TV the doorbell rang. Despite all his best intentions, he couldn't help hoping it was Zoe. Almost as much as he hoped it wasn't.

He opened the door to find a pet carrier on the doorstep. A note was stuck to the top: "Because someone needs to look out for you."

He stared through the wire at Little Dude's small furry body, then he walked out to the driveway then into the street. He wanted a glimpse of her, that was all. Halfway up the block, a car pulled out from the curb. He watched until she turned the corner, then returned to his house and his new cat.

That night he lay in bed with Little Dude's tiny claws kneading his shoulder. The myriad pinpricks were nothing compared to the ache in his chest.

On Wednesday he phoned Jacinta to get another third-person update on how Zoe was doing. It wasn't enough and he wound up calling Tom again. He knew it was tragic, but he couldn't stop himself. If he couldn't have her in his life, at least he could know that she was doing okay.

Both Jacinta and Tom assured him that was the case, that Zoe seemed solid and on top of things. Liam wanted to shake them both, remind them that Zoe was a master at stuffing her feelings down deep and ignoring them. He wanted to demand one of them go to her at night to make sure she wasn't drinking herself to sleep and that she was eating properly. God knew, he wasn't, and he didn't have the luxury of anesthetizing himself with alcohol.

But not knowing what was going on with Zoe was going to be the hard reality of his life. He might as well get used to it. That night he gave in to the urge that had been dogging him all week and brought the painting of Zoe back into the house.

He hung it above his bed, even though he knew it was dumb and torturous. Between Little Dude and the painting, he at least had the illusion that she was in his life.

Thursday afternoon he was contemplating the joys of his first weekend without Zoe when he heard the steady, measured tap-tap of boot heels on concrete. He knew before he swiveled in his office chair who it was.

Sure enough, there she was, standing in his doorway. He drank in the sight of her—long legs in dark denim, a black T-shirt stretched over her breasts. Her hair was loose around her shoulders, her hands tucked into the pockets of a black leather bomber jacket.

His chest tightened.

Damn, she looked good. She looked like the best thing under the sun.

Her gaze was steady as it met his. "Hi."

For a second he couldn't speak. Then he found his voice. "Zoe."

She stepped over the threshold into his office.

"Bummer about the biker comp. Vinnie tells me we were robbed."

"Vinnie's a little biased. I've already had eight phone calls from people who saw our bike, so the comp served its purpose. You're going to be busy."

"Good. How's Little Dude?"

"Hungry. Demanding. Yet to be litter trained."

"I knew you two were made for each other."

She dropped into the seat opposite him and met his eyes squarely. "I don't suppose you've come to your senses yet?"

He didn't bother answering. He studied her face. "You look good."

"Do I? I feel like shit. Can't sleep, no appetite. When I do sleep, all I dream about is you," she said matter-of-factly. "But

I'm guessing you know what that's like." Her green eyes were challenging.

"It'll get easier," he said.

"What if I don't want it to? What if I don't want to stop loving you, Liam Masters?"

He stared at her. She had no idea how much he'd wanted to hear her say those words again. Even though he knew they wouldn't get either of them anywhere, he still wanted to hear the words.

"It's for the best," he said, his mouth dry.

"Bullshit. You and I have wanted each other since we were kids. That kind of feeling doesn't fade away, Liam. It stays with you your whole life. It's rare and it's precious and I'm damned if I'm going to give up on you without a fight."

Her eyes flashed and her cheeks were pink with emotion. He wanted to kiss her so badly it hurt.

"You can't change what I am," he said.

She leaned forward, her face intense.

"I don't want to change what you are. You're an amazing man. Beautiful, generous, kind, honorable. You're nothing like your father, Liam. I know he hurt you, I know you have scars on the inside as well as the outside, but you are not him. You could never be him. You've spent your whole life making sure that would never happen. Do you really have that little faith in yourself?"

"You saw what I did to Marty Johannsen. I was out of control, Zoe. If that bouncer hadn't pulled me off him, God knows what would have happened."

"You would have stopped."

"You know that for certain, do you? Because I don't."

He stared at her, grim. She held his eye.

"I know it, because I know you."

He shook his head. "I saw your eyes, Zoe. I saw the way

you looked at me afterward. You were right to be afraid of me. Smart. Smarter still to keep your distance."

She frowned as though she couldn't believe what she was hearing.

"Afraid of you? I wasn't afraid of you, Liam. I was afraid *for* you. The police were on their way, you had blood on your face, some huge damned bouncer had you in a headlock. I was terrified for you."

He stared at her, saw the unflinching truth in her eyes. He sat back in his chair, blinking rapidly to clear his vision.

Zoe watched him patiently, a small frown between her eyebrows.

"Don't let him do this to you, Liam. You and your mom survived so much. Your injuries, the escape. You made a new life for yourselves. And when she was gone, you kept surviving on your own. Everything around us is a testament to the power of your will and the goodness and strength in you. Can't you see that?"

He wanted to believe what she was saying. He wanted relief from the ache in his chest that had settled there since he sent her out of his life. He wanted to wake to Zoe every day for the rest of his life.

He pushed back his chair and stood. He was trying to do the right thing here, protect her. Why couldn't she see that?

"You don't know what it's like to be afraid of someone who's supposed to love you," he said.

"I know that."

"Do you? You know what it's like to lie in bed at night and nearly piss yourself when you hear his footsteps on the front path? You know what it's like to hear your mom screaming for help and to know that no one will ever answer her? Do you have any idea what that feels like, Zoe?" he demanded. He was yelling, his hands shaking.

Zoe looked at him, compassion in her eyes. "No. But I know what it's like to believe you're broken, that something inside me isn't enough. I know what it's like to be scared of living."

He swore, long and loud. "I'm not afraid. Jesus Christ, can't you see that this is the only way?"

He felt as though he was clutching at straws, as though any moment he was going to give in to the need to hold her and touch her and then they would both be lost because he wouldn't have the will to let her go again.

"You're not your father, Liam," she said. "I know you believe you are, that the anger in you came from him, but it's not true. You're entitled to be pissed at life. You got dealt a shitty, shitty hand. If you didn't raise hell when you were a kid, it would have been a bloody miracle. When I think of all the people who have let you down over the years, all the people who should have stepped in and stopped what was happening, it makes me want to punch a hole in the wall. But just because you're angry doesn't make you your father. Not by a long shot."

He stared at her, exhausted. She didn't understand. Maybe she couldn't. It was up to him to protect her.

"You don't know that," he said wearily.

"I do. But you don't. Not yet, anyway."

She stood and pulled a folded piece of paper from her back pocket. He frowned as she passed it to him. He stared at the address scrawled across the page.

"He's still alive. He lives in a trailer park outside of Brisbane. He works as a mechanic," she said.

He went cold. He shook his head. He could feel Zoe watching him.

"Go talk to him, Liam," she said. "Go see for yourself who he is and who you are."

To his great shame, a wash of fear tightened his gut at the mere thought of being in the same room as his father. He took a step backward, shaking his head.

"No. I don't need to see him to know what he is."

Zoe moved closer. She reached out to fold her hands over his as he gripped the piece of paper.

"Please, Liam. Please do this. For yourself, for us. I love you so much and I know you love me."

He stared into her eyes, seeing the love and the will and the hope there.

"Please do this one thing for me. And if you still feel the same after you see him, I'll back off. You'll never hear from me again," she promised.

He thought about what she was asking. Then he thought about all that she'd said to him, about how much he wanted to believe what she was saying. He'd always believed it was impossible to drown out the memory of his mother's screams, that remembering them kept him strong and resolute. But what if Zoe was right? What if he could have what he wanted—her in his life, his bed, his heart? What if he didn't have to be alone?

"There's a flight to Brisbane first thing tomorrow. We could be there and back in one day," she said.

He shook his head. There was no way he was taking her within a mile of his old man. Hell would freeze over before he let that happen.

"If I go, I go alone," he said.

Zoe frowned. He waited for her to argue, but she was simply quiet for a moment before she nodded.

"Okay. If that's what you want," she said.

"It is," he said.

She nodded and moved to his desk, reaching for the mouse on his computer.

"I'll book your flight."

He watched as she tapped away at the computer.

Tomorrow he would see his father for the first time in more than twenty years. The thought made his gut churn.

He started to pace, unable to stand still. Useless to pretend that he wasn't scared. Rationally he knew he could take anything his father threw at him. Graham Masters would be in his fifties now, and years of alcohol abuse would have taken their toll. Liam was younger, stronger, fitter. But it was impossible to get past the fear that had been bred into his bones where his father was concerned.

He tried to imagine the scenario in his head, what he'd say to his father, what his father might say back, but he drew a blank. The truth was, he'd never even contemplated making contact with his brutal parent. He'd simply channeled all his energies into escaping him.

And now he was coming full circle.

Zoe moved to collect a page from the printer.

"You leave at six, arrive at nine. I booked you a rental car at the airport," she said as she handed him his flight confirmation.

She cupped his cheek in her hand.

"I know this is hard, but it's worth it," she said.

He stared at her, hope warring with fear and doubt.

He wanted her to be right. He didn't want to contemplate the alternative.

BY THE TIME the plane landed in Brisbane the following morning Liam's agitation had settled into a grim determination. He had no idea what to expect. He was doing this for Zoe. He didn't let himself think beyond that very simple motivation.

He hadn't been to Brisbane since he and his mom fled. For obvious reasons, the place held no appeal for him as an adult.

In the back of his mind there had always been the thought that he might run into his father if he set foot in the city again.

He forced himself to look around as he drove alongside the Brisbane River. The sun was shining, the city looked prosperous. It was a place, like any other. At least, that was what he told himself.

His grip tightened on the steering wheel as he neared the southwestern suburb of Inala. This was where they had lived for much of his eight years with his father, moving from one rental property to the next. He hadn't been surprised to learn his father still worked in the area. Graham Masters had always been a creature of habit.

Liam had to use the street directory to find Robard and Son Mechanics, the motor garage where his father worked. He parked out the front of a shabby cinder-block building, eyeing the garage's faded signage and the rusting car hulks on the asphalt pad out front.

He wiped his hands on the seat of his jeans before heading for the door marked Reception. A bell rang as he entered, and a thin, gray-haired man standing behind the front counter looked up from a stack of invoices. Liam studied the man's prominent cheekbones and big nose, noting his grease-stained overalls. Not his father. Not unless his memory had really done a number on him over the years. His gaze dropped to the name embroidered above the man's heart: Keith. Definitely not his father, then.

"G'day. How can I help you?" Keith asked, pushing his paperwork to one side.

Liam forced air into his lungs.

"I'm looking for Graham Masters," he said.

"Graham? Sure. I'll go get him."

The other man gave Liam a curious head-to-toe before disappearing through a doorway that Liam assumed led to the workshop.

Liam took a deep breath and wiped his hands on his jeans again. His breakfast sat like a lump in his stomach and he turned to study the old motor parts calendars and posters on the wall, looking for distraction. His eye was caught by a wall of certificates, proud evidence that the mechanics at Robard and Son made a point of keeping up with their training. He moved to stand in front of the one certificate with his father's name on it. He was still staring at the faded print when he heard the scuff of footsteps behind him.

"Better not be trying to sell me anything, not when I'm in the middle of cleaning out a fuel injector," a voice said.

Low and deep, it was terrifyingly familiar. Every muscle in Liam's body tensed. His hands curled into fists. A rush of anger, decades old, roared through him.

Jesus, how he hated this man. The feeling was hot and visceral, burning its way through his body. The impulse to punish and destroy that came hard on its heels was almost undeniable. He was a man now, not a child. He could give as good as he got. More, even. He could serve up what his father had dished out so easily, smash his father into oblivion, make him hurt and bleed until he was begging for mercy, the way he'd made Liam and his mother beg for mercy all those years ago.

Suddenly Liam understood one of the reasons why he'd been so scared of coming here today. Yes, he was afraid of his father, but he was more afraid of himself, of what he might do to the man who had beaten his wife and child so relentlessly year after year.

"Well, you want to talk to me or what? Ain't got all day, you know," his father said from behind him.

Liam forced his hands to soften, made a conscious effort to relax his shoulders. Then he turned and met his father's eyes for the first time in more than twenty years.

And felt a chill race up his spine. Because he could have been staring into his own eyes. The same color, the same shape, sitting in a face that was also disturbingly familiar. The square jaw, the cheekbones, the nose—they were the same features he stared at every morning when he shaved.

Talk about a chip off the old block.

"Jesus Christ almighty," Graham Masters said, shaking his head from side to side. "Look what the cat dragged in!"

Liam had no time to think as his father stepped forward, his hand extended. Before he knew what he was doing, Liam was having his hand pumped enthusiastically, and his father was slapping him on the arm.

"This is unbelievable," his father said. "Unbelievable. After all these years."

He turned to Keith, who was hovering curiously.

"This is my boy!" Graham said. "Lost, all these years. But I always knew he would find me. That's why I stayed around the old stomping ground, so he'd be able to find me when he came looking."

Liam stared at his father, barely able to comprehend his words. This was the man who had put out cigarettes on his body. The man who'd kicked him until his ribs broke. The man who'd clipped him across the ear so brutally that his eardrum had burst from the impact. Standing here, clapping Liam on the back. Tears, for God's sake, glistening in his father's eyes.

"Just woke up one day and they were gone," Graham explained to Keith. "Bitch stole off with him in the night. Never could find where she'd gone." He wiped his eyes on his sleeve. "Still, you're here now, right? Come looking for your old man."

He reached out to clap Liam on the back again, but Liam caught his arm before he could make contact.

There was a moment of taut suspense as they locked eyes. Then Liam released his grip and his father snatched his hand back.

"What's up your ass?" Graham Masters asked, casting a look toward Keith, embarrassed the other man had witnessed the fraught moment.

"What do you reckon?" Liam asked.

Again they locked gazes and his father was the one to break the contact.

"Look, I don't want any trouble," his father said. "If that's what you're here for, you can piss off."

"What's wrong, Dad? Not so keen to take a shot when the odds are a little more even?" Liam asked.

"I don't know what kind of rubbish your mother's been filling your head with, but I don't have time for this."

Graham turned to walk away but Liam blocked his path. His father kept his eyes on the floor. Liam could see a muscle working in his jaw.

It took a moment for Liam to recognize the emotion thrumming through the other man's body. Then he got it: his father was scared of him. His father was so scared he didn't dare move, worried he'd trigger a confrontation that was bound to turn ugly.

Liam stared down at his father's head, registering for the first time that he topped him by a good two or three inches. He was bigger in the shoulders, too, and deeper in the chest. He had no doubt that he could take his father apart, piece by piece. His father knew it, too.

"You're scared of me," Liam stated.

His father's eyes flicked sideways and he forced a laugh.

"Nothing to be scared of. Don't know why you're being so damned surly," Graham said.

"Don't you? Maybe I'm a little bent out of shape about the

way you used to beat the crap out of me and Mom when I was a kid. What do you think?"

His father glanced toward Keith again, clearly acutely aware of the other man playing witness to their confrontation.

"Look, I don't want no trouble," his father said.

"Too late," Liam said quietly.

His father was sweating, beads standing out on his pale brow.

"I've got a heart condition," he said. "I'm not supposed to get wound up."

"Yeah? Mom had a broken jaw and a ruptured spleen. Didn't stop you from laying into her again." Righteous fury and a heady sense of power filled Liam. To see his father so reduced, sweating with fear—it was the antidote to every nightmare from his childhood, the ultimate revenge fantasy.

Graham's chest heaved and his eyes grew shiny. Liam realized his father was about to cry. He should have relished the moment, gloried in it. His father reduced to tears and sniveling within the space of a few minutes. Liam couldn't have scripted it better.

Instead it filled him with a rush of disgust and pity.

Because his father *was* pitiful, standing there hunched and scared because his long-lost son had dared to confront him with the truth.

"You're pathetic," Liam said. He stepped back, releasing his father from their standoff.

His father's hands were shaking as he raised them to push his hair back. Liam recognized the gesture as one of his own, but this time it didn't send a chill through him.

"You're a bully," he said slowly. It amazed him he'd never seen it before. His father had loomed so large in his memories, so unstoppable and all powerful that Liam had never taken the step back required to see him through an adult's eyes.

He'd spent so much of his life being afraid of his own impulses, particularly his anger. And all the time he'd been operating under a misconception. He'd thought his father was a strong man, a powerful man with no impulse control. But he wasn't. Graham Masters was weak. He was a bully who had subjugated his wife and child because he'd had precious little power in the real world. He was a man who crumbled at the first sign of real opposition, a man who couldn't even meet his son's eyes and face the truth that lay between them.

Liam ran his hand over his face. He felt as though an enormous weight had lifted from his shoulders. This was what Zoe had wanted him to see. She'd said it, hadn't she? *Go see for yourself who he is and who you are.* Because she'd known, and she'd tried to tell him, but he hadn't been able to see it for himself.

Liam turned for the door. He was halfway through when his father spoke.

"That's it? You're just going?"

Liam didn't bother replying. He strode to the car, started the engine and pulled out into the street.

And all the while one thought was turning over and over in his mind: Zoe.

Zoe, the brave. Zoe, the infuriating. Zoe, the sexy. Zoe, the love of his life. Zoe, the woman he was no longer afraid to love.

He'd almost lost her, but she'd saved him from himself. Now all he wanted was to find her and haul her into his arms and hold her for the rest of his life.

Adrenaline pumping through him, he stepped on the gas. He couldn't get home fast enough.

ZOE CHECKED HER WATCH for the hundredth time. She'd done the calculations, factoring in traffic and unfamiliar roads. By her figuring, Liam should have been with his father for an hour by now.

She wondered what was happening, how he was feeling. She'd wanted to go with him so badly. When he'd insisted on going alone, it had killed her to bite her tongue. But she'd known she was asking him to step way outside of his comfort zone. Only her personal plea had pushed him into agreeing to confront his past in the first place. She had decided to be content with that. Then she'd booked herself a seat on the flight that left after Liam's, and this morning she'd followed him up to Brisbane. She'd been hanging around the airport for nearly two hours now, waiting for him to return from meeting his father, wanting to be there for him if he needed her.

It had taken all week for her to find Graham Masters's contact details. Simply finding his first name had been a major production, involving reaching out to her mother for the first time in a long while, then roping her into unearthing old paperwork from storage. Then Zoe had tried the Internet for a phone listing, but Liam's father was either unlisted or not interested in communicating with the world via phone. Eventually she'd leaned on a former client who had joined the police force. It had taken three days and some interjurisdictional tap-dancing, but eventually he'd gotten back to her with Graham Masters's work and home details.

She'd done all she could do. The rest was up to Liam. She had great faith. He was a smart, perceptive man. He would take one look at his father and understand that they were about as unlike as two people could be, regardless of genetics, regardless of nature/nurture, regardless of anything.

An announcement came over the loudspeaker and Zoe glanced anxiously at the departure display again. Liam's return flight didn't leave for another three hours but there was a direct flight to Melbourne every hour. If Liam finished early, he could switch to any one of them. Even though she'd positioned herself on the main causeway, she might miss him.

She forced herself to pick up her book again. If she missed Liam, she would see him in Melbourne. It wasn't the end of the world. It only felt like it right now because she knew he was dealing with the most challenging confrontation of his life and she wasn't there to support him.

She glanced one more time up the causeway before trying to concentrate on her book and caught sight of a tall, broad-shouldered figure striding toward the departure gates.

Liam.

Her heart thumped against her rib cage as she shot to her feet. His face was set, unreadable.

Oh, God. What if her idea had backfired? What if seeing his father had only further entrenched his belief that he was his father's son?

She left the waiting area and stepped onto the causeway. She kept her gaze fixed on Liam's face as he approached, deciding to wait until he got closer to draw his attention by calling to him.

Suddenly she felt stupid for trailing him to Brisbane and haunting the airport to lie in wait for him. She should have waited in Melbourne, let him come to her in his own time. She'd been so determined to be there for him in some way that she'd convinced herself this was the sensible thing to do. But if things had gone badly, if he needed time to sort himself out, she was the last person he'd want to see.

She was about to retreat and hide behind her book when Liam's gaze slid over her briefly before coming back for a second look.

Her heart seemed to stop in her chest as recognition dawned on his face. He smiled, a slow, devastating smile that made parts of her melt on the spot. Then he was striding toward her. She lengthened her stride to meet him halfway, almost breaking into a run.

"Liam—" The rest of her words were swallowed by his mouth as he kissed her, his arms sliding around her to haul her close.

She sank into the hardness of his chest, letting her hips and thighs press against his. His fingers curled into her body, holding her so tightly it almost hurt.

She didn't give a damn. Every question she had, every doubt, every concern was swept away by his kiss.

It seemed like a long time before they came up for air. Liam framed her face with his hands and pressed his forehead against hers, his eyes closed. She felt the intensity in him, knew he was having a silent communion with himself. She could guess what he was thinking: *this is right, this is perfect and it's mine.*

She knew, because it was exactly what she was thinking.

"Zoe Ford, I love you," he said when he opened his eyes.

It was the first time he'd said it to her, and she was surprised by how much the affirmation meant.

"I love you, too, Liam Masters."

He looked into her eyes, his thumbs caressing her cheeks.

"Thank you," he said, his voice very deep.

She frowned, shook her head slightly.

"For what?"

"For setting me free," he said.

Tears filled her eyes and he caught them with his thumbs as they fell onto her cheeks.

"You idiot. I was just returning the favor," she said.

He smiled and she smiled back.

"Move in with me?" he asked.

"Only if you marry me," she countered.

His smile widened into a grin. "Ms. Ford, so forward."

"Always and forever, and don't you forget it."

His grin faded and he studied her face as though he was trying to memorize it.

"Yes," he said after a long moment. "Absolutely. As soon as possible."

She kissed him, offering up her heart and soul along with her mouth and body. Then she stepped away from him and grabbed his hand.

"Come on," she said, leading him back the way he'd come.

"The departure gates are that way," he said, pointing in the opposite direction.

"Yeah, but the Airport Hilton is this way."

He was a smart man; he didn't need further explanation. Within ten minutes they were checked in and in the elevator, kissing each other like wild things. Liam barely got the door open before she had his jeans unzipped. Time blurred after that as they tore at each other's clothes until she was naked and he was inside her, stroking them both to fulfillment.

It had been a whole week since she'd had his hands on her body. She came explosively, his name on her lips. He smiled and looked into her eyes as he stroked into her some more, then it was his turn to shudder and lose himself.

He pulled her against him afterward, cradling her against his chest. She waited until their heartbeats had returned to normal before speaking.

"Do you want to talk about it?" she asked.

He kissed the top of her head, smoothed his hand down her back.

"There's not much to say. He's old and gray but he looks like me. Or, I guess, I look like him."

She knew how much Liam would hate that, and she pressed a kiss onto his chin.

"He tried to pretend like it was some big old homecoming, as though I'd been stolen from him," Liam continued. "He didn't like it when I challenged him."

His gaze became distant. She smoothed a hand across his chest.

"He tried to leave and I wouldn't let him. He started to cry, he was so scared of me, Zoe. Big, bad Graham Masters, shaking like a leaf."

"You're his equal now. He's a bully—he doesn't like those odds," she said quietly.

"No." He huffed out a laugh, shook his head. "I didn't realize."

"I know."

He touched her cheek. She turned her face to kiss his palm.

"Pretty stupid, huh?" he said.

She shook her head. Then she slid on top of him so that she was staring down into his beautiful, strong face.

"Not stupid. Understandable. No one survives a childhood like that without scars, Liam."

He nodded. "I was always determined to put it behind me, not let it affect me. I didn't want it to be the most important thing in my life."

"It isn't. But it doesn't mean it didn't happen, either."

He lifted his head to kiss her.

"How did you get so wise?" he asked.

"I'm not wise. I'm the queen of denial, remember? But someone once told me that I was beautiful and special, and I decided to believe him."

"Now, see, that's wise," he said approvingly.

"No, wise is marrying you before you realize you could have anyone now you've slain your dragons," she said.

She was only joking, but Liam's expression became very serious very quickly.

"Zoe Ford, don't you get it? I don't want anyone else. It's always been you, since I saw you standing in your parents' kitchen."

"Yeah? Then what's taken you so long?"

He smiled, all his love for her there in his eyes.

"I'm a slow learner. But once I get the hang of something, I know how to make up for lost time," he said.

"Promises, promises."

"I'm good for it," he said.

"Yeah?"

"Hell, yeah."

And he set about proving it to her.

* * * * *

"I'm the illegitimate daughter of notoriously scandalous parents, Mr. Milford. Candidates for my hand are unlikely to be lining up at the gates."

"Don't be so quick to discount your charms, my dear. Or the charm of your substantial dowry. Or even your brothers' influence. There are as many reasons to marry as there are marriages."

Annalise snorted. "Oh, yes. Perhaps I shall marry for dynastic reasons, or perhaps for property or influence. After all, a loveless, practical marriage worked out so well for my mother."

"Well, you've routed me on that one. I can think of no suitable rejoinder." Ned rose to his feet and extended his hand. "And since that is the case, let me be the first to wish you a long and happy spinsterhood."

Her mouth gaped open. And then she laughed.

And he froze.

This was the first time, Ned realized. The first time he'd seen her eyes light up and her mouth curl. The first time he'd witnessed her features melded together in glorious accord to produce exquisite beauty.

Unbelievable what a change came over her face. Unheard of what effect her throaty, rasping laughter had on his body. It pounded a beat upon his ear, quickly taken up by his pulse. It echoed through him, finally residing in his stirring nether regions.

So easily she did it, awakened these sensations within him—without any apparent effort at all. And she had called him potentially dangerous? Clearly the intelligent thing for him to do would be to steer clear, to leave her to the tender ministrations of Lord Peter Blackthorne.

"You were right." She smiled up at him as she took his hand and climbed to her feet. "I do feel better."

Ah, well. When had he ever chosen the intelligent path?

He did not relinquish her hand. He used it to pull her in, close enough that he could feel the warmth of her. "At the risk of repeating Lord Peter's mistake and anticipating too much—may I ask if you'll be my partner in battledore tomorrow?"

Her smiled dimmed. Her breath came a little faster. His own had gone shallow, as if he'd just run a race—and lost. He ran his gaze over the appealing lift of her brow and the curious angle of her chin. His index finger twitched.

"I should like that," she said.

His finger trembled again and he lifted it, traced the pink and tender shell of her ear, the unique sweep of her jaw. Her pulse leaped beneath her skin, triggering his own. Slowly he tilted her chin up, waiting for her to object, to step back, to slap his hand away.

She did none of those eminently sensible things. Which left him free to do the entirely impractical thing.

Baby soft, the skin of her lips. Her whole body trembled when he touched her there.

He leaned in. Her eyes closed, even as she stood straight

against him, strung as tight as a bow. He pressed his mouth to hers. It was a soft kiss, sweet and chaste. And yet he was hot and hard and as ready as he'd ever been in his life.

She drew back a little. Sighed. Their breath mingled a moment before she slowly backed away.

"Oh," she breathed. Her dark eyes were full of wonder and something that looked like fear. He took a step toward her, but she only shook her head. His outstretched hand fell to his side as she turned to disappear into the wood. This was the first time, Ned realized. The first time, since he'd come to the house party at Welbourne Manor, that he'd seen her eyes light up.

* * * * *

*Follow Ned and Annalise's story in May 2009
in THE DIAMONDS OF WELBOURNE MANOR.
Available May 2009 from Harlequin® Historical.*

*Available in the series romance section,
or in the historical romance section,
wherever books are sold.*

We'll be spotlighting a different series
every month throughout 2009
to celebrate our 60th anniversary.

Look for Harlequin® Historical in May!

Celebrations begin with
a sumptuous Regency house party!

Join three scandalous sisters in

**THE DIAMONDS OF
WELBOURNE MANOR**

Glittering, scintillating, sensual fun
by Diane Gaston, Deb Marlowe
and Amanda McCabe.

**60 years of Harlequin,
600 years of romance
in Harlequin Historical!**

Harlequin® Historical
Historical Romantic Adventure!

If you enjoyed reading
Joanne Rock in the
Harlequin® Blaze™ series,
look for her new book
from Harlequin® Historical!

THE KNIGHT'S RETURN
Joanne Rock

Missing more than his memory,
Hugh de Montagne sets out to find his
true identity. When he lands in a small
Irish kingdom and finds a new liege in the
Irish king, his hands are full with his new
assignment: guarding the king's beautiful,
exiled daughter. Sorcha has had her heart
broken by a knight in the past. Will she be
able to open her heart to love again?

Available April
wherever books are sold.

High rollers, high stakes
and a killer fashion sense.

Three sexy new mysteries from

STEPHANIE
BOND

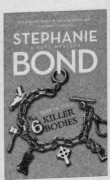

April 2009   May 2009   June 2009

"Bond keeps the pace frantic, the plot tight
and the laughs light."
–*Publishers Weekly*, starred review,
on *Body Movers: 2 Bodies for the Price of 1*

REQUEST YOUR FREE BOOKS!

2 FREE NOVELS
PLUS 2
FREE GIFTS!

HARLEQUIN®
Blaze
Red-hot reads!

YES! Please send me 2 FREE Harlequin® Blaze™ novels and my 2 FREE gifts (gifts are worth about $10). After receiving them, if I don't wish to receive any more books, I can return the shipping statement marked "cancel." If I don't cancel, I will receive 6 brand-new novels every month and be billed just $4.24 per book in the U.S. or $4.71 per book in Canada. Shipping and handling is just 25¢ per book. That's a savings of 15% or more off the cover price! I understand that accepting the 2 free books and gifts places me under no obligation to buy anything. I can always return a shipment and cancel at any time. Even if I never buy another book, the two free books and gifts are mine to keep forever.

151 HDN ERVA   351 HDN ERUX

Name	(PLEASE PRINT)	
Address		Apt. #
City	State/Prov.	Zip/Postal Code

Signature (if under 18, a parent or guardian must sign)

Mail to the **Harlequin Reader Service:**
IN U.S.A.: P.O. Box 1867, Buffalo, NY 14240-1867
IN CANADA: P.O. Box 609, Fort Erie, Ontario L2A 5X3

Not valid to current subscribers of Harlequin Blaze books.

Want to try two free books from another line?
Call 1-800-873-8635 or visit www.morefreebooks.com.

* Terms and prices subject to change without notice. Prices do not include applicable taxes. N.Y. residents add applicable sales tax. Canadian residents will be charged applicable provincial taxes and GST. Offer not valid in Quebec. This offer is limited to one order per household. All orders subject to approval. Credit or debit balances in a customer's account(s) may be offset by any other outstanding balance owed by or to the customer. Please allow 4 to 6 weeks for delivery. Offer available while quantities last.

Your Privacy: Harlequin Books is committed to protecting your privacy. Our Privacy Policy is available online at www.eHarlequin.com or upon request from the Reader Service. From time to time we make our lists of customers available to reputable third parties who may have a product or service of interest to you. If you would prefer we not share your name and address, please check here. ☐

HP

HARLEQUIN *Blaze*

COMING NEXT MONTH

Available April 28, 2009

#465 HOT-WIRED Jennifer LaBrecque
From 0–60
Drag racer/construction company owner Beau Stillwell has his hands full trying to mess up his sister's upcoming wedding. The guy just isn't good enough for her. But when Beau meets Natalie Bridges, the very determined wedding planner, he realizes he needs to change gears and do something drastic. Like drive sexy, uptight Natalie absolutely wild...

#466 LET IT RIDE Jillian Burns
What better place for grounded flyboy Cole Jackson to blow off some sexual steam than Vegas, baby! Will his campaign to seduce casino beauty Jordan Brenner crash and burn, once she discovers what he really wants to bet?

#467 ONCE A REBEL Debbi Rawlins
Stolen from Time, Bk. 3
Maggie Dawson is stunned when the handsomest male *ever* appears from the future, insisting on her help! Cord Braddock's out of step in the 1870s Wild West, although courting sweet, sexy Maggie comes as naturally to him as the sun rising over the Dakota hills....

#468 GOING DOWN HARD Tawny Weber
When Sierra Donovan starts receiving indecent pictures of herself—with threats attached—she knows she's going to need help. But the last person she needs it from is sexy security expert Reece Carter. Although, if Sierra's back has to be against the wall, she can't think of anyone she'd rather put her there....

#469 AFTERBURN Kira Sinclair
Uniformly Hot!
Air force captain Chase Carden knows life will be different now that he's back from Iraq—he's already been told he'll be leading the Thunderbird Squadron. Little does he guess that his biggest change will come in the person of Rina McAllister, his last one-night stand...who's now claiming to be his wife!

#470 MY SEXY GREEK SUMMER Marie Donovan
A wicked vacation is what Cara Sokol has promised herself, although she has to ~~~ entity a secret! Hottie Yannis Petridis is exactly what she's looking for ~~~ od with secrets—he's got one of his own!